Fresh Air
and
Empty Streets

Fresh Air and Empty Streets

Published by Oliver Cable, London.
© 2016 by Oliver Cable. All rights reserved.

First Edition

Cover artwork by Ron Wiessner
Cover design by Mark Ecob

www.CableWrites.com
Oliver@CableWrites.com

ISBN: 9780995450905

Printed and bound in Great Britain by Clays

Fresh Air
and
Empty Streets

Oliver Cable

To whoever finds this book: read it, cherish it, then pass it on.

Happy reading.

16/04/19

TOOTING

ABOUT THE AUTHOR

Oliver Cable was born to English parents in Holland and currently lives in London. As a result, he's not entirely sure where he's from. In the ten years since writing his first poem, he's written short-form poetry and prose, inspired and influenced by jazz, travel and the absurdity of daily life. After following a Creative Writing course at UEA, he turned his hand to writing longer pieces, but to this day still enjoys a good four-line poem.

Fresh Air and Empty Streets is his debut novel.

Thank you to Ron and Stephanie, my partners-in-crime on that first Paris trip. Thanks also to Lantei, who kept the pressure on and the motivation high to keep writing and eventually publish the book.

Thank you Ron also for the endless jazz nights, late-night brainstorms and never-ending edits to the painting that graces the cover of this book.

Thanks to Rebecca and Mark for their patience in turning my book from a handful of handwritten pages to the book you now hold in your hand.

Thanks to Ann and Neil for their boundless support and Constance for your love and wisdom.

Thank you to all my readers.

Paris sparkled like a cloth made of stars, as Felix sat, head in his hands, retching. Behind him, the glorious Sacré-Cœur watched over the city, as the night's cocktail rushed through his stomach and out over the marble steps. A hum hung over Montmartre as hundreds of youth sat around the hill, cigarette smoke and revelry echoing up into the night sky. At times, the sound was punctuated by a beer bottle cascading down the steps and rolling to a stop, unbroken, on the cobbles at the bottom. Tourists sat side by side with like-minded locals, bonding over drinks bought off beer merchants who delivered straight to their thirsty feet. A thousand pinpricks of light drew the outline of a capital city far below. But Felix didn't notice any of this.

He spat, his whole body aching from the strain. The exertion had exhausted him to the point that he felt a longing to sleep right here on these stairs, safe under the watchful domes of the basilica. An unseen car rumbled by on the cobbles, sounding in Felix's mind like a far-off announcement of thunder. He knew a storm was coming – coming since he'd walked out of the house with his bag slung over his shoulder and had boarded that bus. It was brewing, every moment that he walked the streets of this city, increasing in intensity with every further second he spent away from home. He'd put cogs in motion that could now not be reversed, broken that which could now no longer be repaired. He rolled his head back on his shoulders, his closed eyes pointing skywards, and breathed out.

*

Roger had been sitting at the bar as Felix arrived at *Le Lion*. He greeted him and thanked him for what he'd done so far.

"Don't thank me yet." It sounded like a premonition.

As the clock shuffled towards the arranged meeting time, Felix had felt apprehension and excitement rising in equal parts. As the minute hand passed the hour, then quarter past on its way down to half past, hope had begun to slip from the pair.

"He's often late," Roger had said by way of reassurance.

They were on their third beer by now.

An hour in, conversation had all but dried up between the unlikely partners. Roger turned to Felix and shook his head.

*

"*Ca va?*"

Two hands grabbed him and yanked him back into the

real world. Felix forced his eyes to refocus as he blinked up into the face of a stranger. Young, Algerian and with a cap on backwards, he stood with a cigarette between his lips, surveying Felix.

"Oui mec, merci." That was a lie. The city lights spun in front of him as his mind grappled with the memory of the dream and the immediate realisation of where he was.

"Tranquille," the man said, then walked off, glancing back a few metres on to check that Felix hadn't slumped back down.

Felix spat once more, trying to purge the taste of tar, sand and French lager that burned in his throat. Inside his head, he said a quick thanks to his fate that Vivienne, his mother, wasn't around to see him like this. His hands found clean marble beside him and he staggered to his feet, watching Paris whizz by as if watching it through a train window. He swayed, stretching his arms out groggily in an attempt to balance himself. His feet filled with lead as he attempted to put them one in front of the other and navigate his way down the steps. What am I doing here? he thought. He was only aware of the groups on the stairs by way of the wall of sound engulfing him, emanating from a car at the bottom. From it pulsated a heavy rhythmic drone, captivating the youth standing around it, talking, dancing, drinking, flirting. As he passed the group, a bottle smashed on the cobbles behind him. Without looking round, he quickened his step.

His mind was still out there, roaming somewhere in the starry night sky, but his body was chained to the streets of Paris, their cobblestones lit up by the streetlight bouncing off the damp streets. He fell into a pace and soon came to Montmartre's *escaliers*, still abuzz with activity. From here, the steps stretched down as far as the eye could see, until they disappeared under the slowly budding boughs of the overhanging trees. He paused briefly at the top, took a breath and started the descent.

*

Roger banged on the dark green door, then waited. Any sounds inside the house were masked by a passing moped, spluttering out a sound like an angry insect. He banged again with his fist, longer this time.

"Alex!" he yelled. A lady walking her dog glanced over disapprovingly from the other side of the road.

There was no answer. Roger took a step back off the pavement and looked up at the second floor where the sash window had been propped open with a jam jar. He yelled again. Still nothing. Felix could imagine a figure, sitting perfectly still on the sofa, feet flat on the ground and hands between his thighs so as not to make a sound, praying they'd go away. Or maybe he wasn't there at all. He was good at not being there.

Roger called up again, more angrily this time, poised at the tipping point of hope and disappointment. The seconds of silence hung in the air as Felix strained to hear the slightest sound from within. When Roger turned to him and shook his head with a grimace, he felt the weight of his own hope tumbling around him.

Slowly they turned and walked down the street.

*

Back on the steps of Montmartre, Felix felt safe, wrapped in the warm street glow as if the city itself had wrapped its arms around him. He was overcome with a clarity of thought, he realised, as clear as the cloudless night sky, that told him he'd succeed, that told him that he *would* meet Alexander. For a moment he felt an absolute unity with his body and his decisions, the clouds in his thoughts blown away and his mind suddenly answering questions as opposed to asking them. No, he realised now, *this* was the way to live, his mind unshackled and his body free to lay itself at the very heart of all the world had to offer. Indeed, as he examined his thoughts from his position high above, he saw them caught within a cage, a miniature jail-cell with bars he had looked straight past until now.

As his legs carried him back along the Boulevard de Clichy, the route home crystal clear in his mind, Parisian nightlife was continuing in earnest. As he passed one of the many sordid clubs, Felix swatted away the approach of a woman outside who clasped herself onto his arm with the promise of *"quelque chose de spécial pour vous."* No, thought Felix, you can't give me what I'm looking for. No one around here can.

Felix's body arrived back at the hotel, and called out to his mind to function. He pressed the buzzer and heard footsteps inside. Within seconds, the smartly-dressed night porter slid the lock and let him in, and Felix found himself tramping the polished floor and then the stairs – *more stairs* – to his room.

His key struggled to find the lock as it clattered around in the gloom, but eventually he slid it home, twisted it and pushed the handle down. The door gave and swung inwards under his dead weight. Inside the room he kicked off his shoes without untying the laces, pulled off his jeans and t-shirt and crashed into bed, clothes left strewn in a pile on the ground.

It would be a good fifteen minutes before his thoughts would leave him alone, but he fairly enjoyed their company. With his eyes closed, hands folded behind his head and his legs crossed at the ankle, he imagined himself in a meadow, high on the wave of a spring about to break and flood the world with summer. He watched as a girl approached, heard himself call this stranger over to join him, and the next thing he knew they were tumbling in grass as high as their happiness, and he'd fallen instantly, madly in love, without realisation, within seconds and far too fast for his mind to stem the flow of romance-fuelled endorphins. As Felix watched himself frolic, he discovered a person capable of a clarity of living so powerful as to rush through, over, all around him like water crashing over rocks, cascading and tumbling down into a semi-conscious glow, falling endlessly into unknown space and –

*

Screeching car brakes. Crashing waves. A woman's

scream.

Felix awoke many hours later to an explosion of noise so complete and so dominating as to be totally disorientating. Bottles rained down from an enormous bin below his window into a rubbish truck, crashing and cascading with such vigour that he could almost see them, green and brown and white all mixed up with reds and blues as colours flashed behind his closed eyelids, dancing and melding into pain as his head throbbed. The curtains he'd neglected to close over the large floor-to-ceiling windows he'd left wide open let in all the light and noise of the street. His body was covered with sweat. Kicking off the duvet, he immediately started to shiver. He pulled it up around his chin again and turned to the cold side of the pillow. His boxers were twisted halfway around his legs and his left thigh was constricted by the sheet, which had wrapped itself around him like a vine. He burrowed deeper into the bed, jamming his face into the pillows to block out the cacophony and shy away from the world, hoping for sleep to come peacefully, hoping to deny his existence in this state and return to his body when it felt less grim.

But it was no good. Drunken daydreams stalked him through worlds of quasi-sleep, their long bony fingers of decay reaching out for his mind, until all he could do was tear open his eyes and confront the morning pain again. So stuck was he in his current state that he didn't even consider closing the blinds or the window. It was easier to suffer in silence, in inaction, in total denial of his situation than to do anything about it. He had crashed hard, a modern-day

Icarus flying too close to the sun. Now his wings had melted he was left with nothing but pain. A voice inside his head, quiet at first but building in intensity as Felix tried harder and harder to quash it, questioned his journey. *"What are you doing here?"* it seemed to ask, *"what do you possibly think you're going to achieve?"* Felix shook his head to shake loose the thought but it persisted. *"Why are you even here? What good is any of this going to do for anyone?"*

He sat up groggily and looked around. What would Vivienne say if she saw this? Half a baguette, by now dry to the point of rock-solid, a chunk of brie with his pocket-knife sticking out of it, a handful of business cards he'd picked up, used metro tickets scattered on the carpet: Felix's room was in about as much of a state as he was. He put his feet down on the carpet, feeling the old, oft-trodden floor hard to his bare soles. He crossed the room to the bathroom, and was taken aback as he caught his reflection in the shower door. His hair stuck up in unruly clumps, shooting off in every which way in a desperate attempt to leave the wasteland that was his body. His eyes were red and sunken into his skull, and his skin, pasty at the best of times, now resembled Arctic snow in the sun.

Without really being aware of his actions, he'd turned the taps on the shower and sent water, fresh water, rushing up the pipe and out of the shower head, purging, cleaning his skin as the water wrapped itself around him like a blanket. For a moment, he considered staying here forever, eternally embraced in the warm, not having to face the world. Eyes shut, he imagined what staying here forever would feel like. He saw a safe, glorious endlessness in which no one expected anything from him, in a society which didn't expect progress, or success, a society which excused him from all responsibility. He found himself relieved at not having to go through with the nerve-wracking meeting he was here to have with Alexander. He could go back to living a life of not knowing, a life where no one kicked at the shins of the status quo.

*

"There is *one* more thing we could try," Roger had said as they sat at a bar on Rue Laplace later that evening. The mood since visiting Alexander's house had been one of extinguished hope, smoked down to the final embers and crushed into the curb. Felix leaned in, eyebrows raised expectantly.

"He runs an art class somewhere in the east of the city. He never really spoke of it, but I know a girl who he used to...who might still go there. I'll ask her about it."

The bar was poky and filling up with smoke from the three men and token woman who sat at the bar lighting each cigarette off the butt of the last. The woman drank pastis that Felix could smell from where he sat. She had a voice like gravel and a newspaper lying beside her. She would periodically pick it up to look at, folding it this way and that in order to find the story she wanted. She never seemed to read for long though before she'd fold it shut and slam it on the bar in disgust at something one of her self-destructive comrades had said, often accompanying the motion with a gritty *"Non, non, **non**!"* and launching into a tirade on some subject or other. Then she'd pick up the paper, unfold it and withdraw into her own world again.

"Sylvene, her name is. I'll drop by this week and pick her brain."

"Why don't you just call?"

"It's better if I go round." Roger said.

"Yeah, better fo-" Felix bit his tongue. Let Roger do what he had to do.

The lady at the bar let out a loud snort, sending smoke shooting out of her nostrils, then got up, moving to the back of the bar and the toilets, shuffling into a table on the way.

Roger signalled to the barman: *"Encore deux."*

*

When Felix dared admit to himself that he could stand in the shower no longer, he composed himself and reached to turn off the water. He stood, head down, too broken to reach for his towel as he felt the water dripping off his chin and running down his legs, *plop plop,* onto the shower floor.

As he went back into his room, he saw a missed call from Roger. He called him back.

"'Allo?" Roger sounded like death.

"It's Felix," he said.

"Ah," Roger said, and was quiet. When Roger still said nothing, Felix prodded him.

"You called."

"Oh yes," a pause, "I met Sylvene last night. She told me where we could find Alexander."

"Great." Apprehension rose in Felix's throat.

"He runs an art class on Tuesdays, down in the 19th arrondissement. Evening time. I'll text you through the address."

"Okay," In his current state, Felix almost forgot his manners. "Oh, and thanks Roger, I appreciate it."

"Keep your thanks for now."

That day Felix forced himself out of his room and walked the streets aimlessly. He had a day to kill in Paris and nothing to do with it. It was one of those days where he was neither there nor not there – a passenger, watching the world float by as if observing from behind steamed up bus windows. A row of tables lined the Place de Clichy, where locals of all ages sat enjoying the sun. Felix pulled back a chair and sat down. A sour-faced waiter came out, grunted at him, and Felix ordered *un café*. The man said nothing and turned to go inside. A good five minutes later, the waiter came out carrying a tiny cup and a glass of water. He put it on Felix's table, looked down as if he had a bad smell under his nose, and walked away. Felix sat and stirred and sipped and stared straight ahead at lives he had not an inkling of. To imagine yesterday he'd been so alive, so himself, so aware and so one with his body. Different story today, wasn't it? He sat with his elbow on the table and his forehead resting in his palm, wishing yesterday's euphoria back yet not strong enough to will it to return. With great highs came great lows.

A car rolled by on the cracked tarmac, painted with official-looking blue and red stripes. As it passed the café, the passenger wound down the window and waved a two-finger salute, yelling incomprehensibly at some faceless target. Visibly relieved by his outburst, he wound the window up again as the driver sped on down the street. A few minutes later an unassuming lady passed by, holding under her arm a large flat package wrapped in brown paper. Following closely behind, a younger girl with sunglasses and an expensive handbag over her shoulder carried a grotesque print of pink high heels. At the table beside him, a woman was interviewing an outspoken young man. It's all a game to you, Felix thought. Nothing matters to any of you here, not like it could end up mattering to me. A loneliness had crept up on him from the darkness of his hangover, questioning again his motives, urging him again to realise what a fool he'd been to even start this pursuit. He started to doubt whether he was living in the same world as those around him. Yes, he sat at a table in a very real square, but did he figure in this society anymore? Was he still capable of interacting, of conversing, of forming a part of Parisian life? What was he but a minute scratch on the surface of the city, itself only a dot on the map? Complete insignificance. He sat and watched his life stretch out ahead of him like a desolate burned-out street of time.

*

As Tuesday came, Felix woke up in a mild state of dread.

Who was he to impose himself on this man's life on some egotistical whim? What right did he have to change this man's life forever with a simple curiosity to meet him? Was this normal social behaviour? Would he one day, perhaps at the end of this very day, look back and feel he'd committed a sin of social interaction? That what was gone should stay gone – that things were the way they were because that was the natural balance?

He spent most of the morning pondering this, locked in his room and locked up in his mind, going over the endless possibilities of the eventual meet-up, with one key thought: was this socially *really* fucked up? Was it weird that he had somehow convinced himself that this was the right way to behave, that this was the correct course of action? He spoke a line from Macbeth out loud, addressing no one but his own thoughts, as an outside voice of reason: *"I am in blood/ Stepped in so far that, should I wade no more/Returning were as tedious as go o'er."* It was no longer a question of social morality, he realised, but a question of no going back. Having come all this way, and having risked ruining his relationship with his mother, he was not now going to give up, right or wrong.

As morning turned to afternoon, Felix decided to explore the 19th before heading to the art class. It would distract him if nothing else. As the *métro* rumbled and crashed around the underbelly of Paris, Felix had accepted whatever his fate might bring. When he left the train at Père Lachaise, he decided he'd done enough worrying. His head was clear and he was ready, hopeful even.

Felix followed the signs to the city's cemetery. A certain peace hung in the air as he wandered amongst the rows and rows of stones, many overgrown and moss-green. Some tombs were elaborate stone structures, standing out many metres above the soil, some with stained-glass windows and rusted iron doors, while many just stood as a single stone in the ground adorned with a name. He sat down with his back to a tree, its cracked bark textured like an elephant's leg, listening to the consuming calm, to the birds chattering in the rustling trees, to the insects buzzing behind his head. It was well and truly spring, he thought. The serenity of the graveyard instilled in him a feeling of profound calm. In the tree above Felix's head, a crow squawked. Far off, another responded. Ahead of him, somewhere, lay the city, obscured by rows of tombstones, trees and high-rise.

As evening fell over the area, Felix made his way towards Rue Alexandre Dumas. He wasn't used to this kind of area, and once or twice caught himself glancing over his shoulder when he heard a noise. He was early, wanting to get there before the class started. Reaching the block, he looked up at the building. Somewhere in there is the man who gave me life, Felix thought, and we're both equally in the dark about how this is going to go. He pressed the buzzer and the door clicked, letting him into a dimly-lit corridor of what might once have been a school. A black-and-white tiled hall forked into two corridors, running off at right-angles from each other. At the end of one was a spiral staircase towards the high ceiling, looking more like a fire escape than a main thoroughfare. A sign next to the stairs pointed up for *"Atelier"* so up Felix climbed, the stairs rattling as he went. The first floor was nothing like the ground. A brightly-coloured mish-mash of furniture met him, looking for all the world like it had been collected from the street. Carpet had been neglected to be laid over the chipboard. In the corner stood a staircase with a thick wooden bannister, supported by a single stump of wood which it was duct-taped onto. Felix crossed, his shoes knocking on the floor, his heart speeding up involuntarily until at least double his pace. With every step his gut clenched as he rode this rollercoaster of expectations. The stairs led to an in-between floor, nothing more than a square room with beanbags and coffee tables. The shapes of people were still visible in their imprints in the seats. Voices drifted down from another set of wooden stairs. He put his hand on the bannister and started climbing.

The floor he emerged onto was abuzz with activity – cigarette smoke mingling and dancing with steam, rising from coffee cups and roll-ups held between outstretched fingers. Felix saw that this art class served an important social function too, nearer a night out at the pub than a lesson in painting. The coffee machine spluttered in the corner, at times audible over the sound of the excited crowd, already sizeable in number, their voices rising and echoing against the high ceiling. So much for getting there early.

A door opened on one side of the corridor and out came a bare-chested man with a red bandana tied round his head, carrying on his shoulder a canvas twice his size. He whistled as he crossed the hall.

"A-tten-tion, les enfants!" he called out. The crowd parted

to let him through. With difficulty he negotiated another doorway and was gone.

Felix looked around hesitantly. Not knowing anyone and not wanting to kick up a scene in front of these strangers, he remained frozen to the spot at the top of the stairs.

"Un enfant perdu!" came a call from beside the coughing coffee machine. Felix looked and saw the man was addressing him. Yes, thought Felix, he certainly felt like a lost child. The man beckoned to him, holding out a steaming brew.

"I'm sorry," Felix said as he approached. He felt he was encroaching on other peoples' territory. *"Je cherche Alexander."* Speaking the name felt alien.

"Alexandre?" The man smiled, pointed at one of the doors in the hall and put up ten fingers, denoting the wait ahead of Felix.

"Merci," Felix muttered as he took the coffee. He moved over to the window with his cup and looked out over the street, a close-up version of what he'd been looking at the night before from the Sacré-Cœur, watching human comings and goings, buses taking a hundred people to a hundred different places. Who they were and what they were doing was a permanent mystery, the same way no one really knew what Felix was doing at the art class. A story couldn't be told from a split-second sighting down a lamp-lit street – lives were just more complex than that, a series of endless human complexities. Who would know looking at Felix that he was en-route to a meeting that would change both his life and that of another man's?

He watched as a passer-by shook hands with the shop

assistant beside a blaze of colours outside the late-night Turkish greengrocer, where fruits lay piled up on racks outside and an artificial glow bathed them from within.

In an instant, a hush fell over the crowd and Felix turned to see that three doors had opened along the corridor. In each doorway stood a single silhouette. The crowd now split and huddled around these three doors, like a congregation around a preacher.

Felix realised he couldn't very well confront the man then and there, so he stayed waiting, watching the shapes step back into their respective classrooms and the crowds outside file in. Everyone seemed to know their place.

In a short time, Felix was alone in the hall. The man who had given him his coffee had indicated the second door, but what was Felix to do? Interrupt the lesson? Wait until Alexander came out? Would he even recognise him from another random art student? Felix's plan had been so straight-forward – go early, meet Alexander, talk things through. Now though, as events had transpired to a completely different scenario, he was locked out of this group for however long the class took and –

"Felix?" Those two hands again, grabbing him and pulling him out of his ruminations. A woman this time, not unattractive, with brown hair that curled around her shoulders.

Taken aback, Felix could only stand there, his mouth slightly open. She held out her hand.

"Sylvene." And suddenly it made sense.

Felix shook her hand. It was soft and cared for, almost

homely.

With a nod of her head, she signalled Felix over to the third door. That hand came out again.

"Wait," she said, the word heavy under a thick French accent. Before Felix could say anything, Sylvene had disappeared into the room and shut the door behind her. His fate was now in this stranger's hands.

A moment later, the door swung open and Felix found himself looking at a reflection of himself, considerably aged by the stress and the lifestyle Alexander had adopted, but recognisable nonetheless. In that split-second before either of them opened their mouths, Felix saw his shaggy brown hair, his dark eyebrows and his height back in the man in front of him.

"Felix." He'd been prepared for this of course – Roger had told him and coaxed him often enough – but to stand face to face with his own flesh and blood for the first time in fifteen years visibly affected him. As they shook hands formally – for how else was one meant to behave with a man you were a blood relative of, yet never really knew? – Felix felt Alexander's hand trembling.

There were a million things to say. So much to say, in fact, that all Felix could muster was:

"Hi."

"Listen," Alexander said. His voice was deep, but not rough, the kind of voice Felix suddenly hoped to grow into. "I've got this class to teach, but then we're off for drinks around the corner. We'll be out in about two hours, if you can wait?"

Felix had been building himself up to this meeting, and to delay it by two hours was an unwelcome hiccup. But what was two hours when he'd been waiting fifteen years?

"It's a place called *Les Deux Peintres* – I'll be there," he said, then added "I promise." There was a certain sadness in his voice, a pleading, the remnants of a wish that things hadn't gone the way they had, a morsel of remorse and a pinch of hope that he could yet fix things up. Or was Felix just imagining all that?

"Okay," Felix said, "I'll see you there."

It had been a strange first meeting.

Alexander cut back into his lesson and proceeded to teach, Felix assumed, as he did every week. Would his behaviour already be different? Would the first meeting and the meeting that was to come be playing on his mind as much as it was on Felix's?

Felix headed towards the stairs, thanking Sylvene, who watched him go. He pushed down and out of the labyrinthine building – bannister creaking, stairs rattling, tiles clicking – and let himself out onto the street.

Felix was momentarily reassured. All he had worried about so far had not materialised. Alexander had been short but not rude – that was just his lack of time. Wasn't it? Either way, he was meeting him later, and now had two hours to himself. After dark, the streets of Paris took on an added glory, even those out in the suburbs. From a run-down area by day rose a warm embracing glow at night. Felix roamed the area, his sense of direction telling him more or less where he had to be later. He found *Les Deux Peintres*, a poky place a single room wide, with paint peeling off its painted front and a few hardy people smoking outside. He'd be back.

An hour and a half later, Felix returned, eager to be there before Alexander. He ordered a *demi-pression* from the barman, a man whose years of loyal service to his patrons was visible on his face. He was presented with a Kronenbourg and took a sip, tasting the foam and then the cold beer slipping down his throat, cold to his insides, coating his stomach in icy relaxation.

There were several high tables free, and Felix placed his coat over a bar stool beside one of them. The walls of the place, once creme-coloured, had been stained a dirty brown by the years of abuse and absorption of life. A few portraits of people Felix didn't recognise hung on the walls, black and white and sepia-tone affairs, the stories of their lives told on their faces. In a far corner was a face he did recognise, as a charcoal drawing of John Coltrane surveyed the room, the paper curling at the edges. He felt at ease. Nobody knew who he was, and Felix liked it that way. There was a complete freedom in being so far away from what he knew – where any mistake would not be held against him and where no one knew what to expect from him, least of all Alexander.

To Alexander, who knew so little about him, he was anyone. He was essentially free to craft whatever personality he wanted to be. He was a slate wiped clean, he figured, by hundreds of miles of rolling bus tyres bringing him deep into a foreign country and to the heart of an unknown city.

What Felix didn't realise was that he was still the same

person, a person he couldn't run away from, no matter how many buses, trains or planes he took. He'd still always be Felix. The only thing wiped clean was others' perception of him.

Alexander was late. Felix had been at the bar for an hour. He was on his third beer when he was challenged to a game of pool by an older man. He initially turned it down, thinking the artists would surely be here soon, but as time wore on, Felix saw he was in for a wait and accepted the old man's invitation. In broken French he chatted to his opponent, who insisted on calling him *jeune-homme* at all times.

"*Et que faites-vous, jeune-homme?*" the old man asked.

"*J'attends quelqu'un.*" Felix responded.

"*Un artiste?*"

"*Oui.*"

The man inhaled through his teeth and winced.

This bar, Felix learned, was an enclave for the area's artists. They came in late, were noisy and didn't always have the money to pay their tabs. The man, clearly practiced after many years spent in this kind of establishment, eyed up his shots quickly, dispatching ball after ball into the pockets. Felix's heart sank with each ball that disappeared down into the depths of the table, their thuds resounding around the quiet room. His opponent had sunk five by the time Felix potted his first. A few moments later, the old man skillfully potted the black to condemn Felix to defeat.

"So, is he here?" the man asked.

"Not yet," Felix had to admit. Then, more to convince

himself than anything else, he added: "But he's coming."

It was nearer eleven when Alexander finally showed up, his buttoned shirt patterned with specks of paint, like hundreds of tiny hot-air balloons on the breeze. As he saw Felix, he held up his hand in a greeting that showed no sign of apology, nor any shame in being so late. More and more people were now entering the bar. Felix thought he recognised some of them from the group he'd seen a few hours before. A lady with neatly permed grey hair stood by the bar and ordered *"un gin-tonique"*, swallowed it in one, then ordered another.

An attractive girl of about Felix's age was the centre of attention for a number of the newcomers. As she played up to it, Felix watched her giggling at the men. Their eyes met for a second, a glint caught in her green eyes. Then Alexander came over, holding two beers. He put them down on the table and shifted a bar stool nearer to the table.

"Hello Felix."

"Hi."

They sat looking at each other in silence for a moment. Alexander was the first to speak.

"Where to start?" he said, speaking Felix's thoughts.

Alexander shook his head and repeated: "Where to start?" The question sounded genuine, as if he honestly didn't have a clue, yet was overlaid with the knowledge that Felix wasn't there for small-talk. He picked the path of his words carefully, cautious of Felix's sentiment towards him.

"First and foremost Felix, I want to be honest with you.

The last thing I want is for you to be walking out of here with any questions. For my part, I'll try and be as clear as possible in what's in my mind still a...let's say, *complex* situation. So please, ask me anything you want."

"Best start at the beginning," Felix said.

"Right," Alexander said. "Yes." He gathered his thoughts and began to speak. "Your mother and I met when we were quite young – she was 18. I must've been 22. My life up until that point had been unremarkable. I was a mediocre student with a few close friends. We all sort of muddled along in life, picking up hobbies, habits and girlfriends along the way. Some stayed, some were temporary. But there was one thing that sort of united us – we were all into our art, in various forms. It was a motley crew of musicians, painters, writers...I suppose that's what kept us all vaguely hanging out together." Alexander took a sip of his beer.

"But yeah, Vivienne," he said, bringing his story back on track. "She was part of a group of friends my lot used to meet up with sometimes. I thought her gorgeous, absolutely beautiful, completely out of my league. Over the course of one night though, we got talking properly, hit it off in a big way and started seeing each other more and more, without the rest of the group." Alexander took on a pensive look. "From there, I guess, we...sort of *happened.*"

Felix listened in silence.

"I couldn't get enough of her. Everything was amazing."

Felix softened as he imagined his mother as a young girl. Then, aware again of where the story was going, stiffened again.

"*We* were amazing. It all just *worked*. I'd spend several nights a week with her and most days too. Until I met her, painting was kind of my...," he paused, "kind of my direction in life. It was what filled my time and cost me my wages. But when I met her, painting took a bit of a back-burner. I had precious little motivation or even time to paint. I suppose I didn't really think anything of it at the time. I was just so blinded by her radiance. We'd talk long into the night, stay up until all hours laughing and just enjoying each others' company, greet the morning and much of the day from under the covers. I suppose I was denying the existence of anything else, except her." Alexander broke off, then changed tack. "You know I painted her once?"

Felix shook his head.

"No, I don't suppose you would know. It's not the kind of thing she'd leave hanging around in the house now. She's probably got it somewhere – bloody hope she has, it took me ages." He looked thoughtful. "Anyway, long story short, she never much liked it. Said it made her look old before her time." He stopped with a wry laugh.

"In a sense I suppose that's how I saw her – four years my junior but far more mature. Dreamt of settling since day one, I think, while I just had my heart set on living. There was so much of the world to see, so much to do. She didn't much like it when I'd crawl into bed next to her after a heavy night's drinking, arriving as the sun was rising, stinking of cigarettes. So *that* stopped." With his index finger, he absent-mindedly drew lines down the condensation on his glass. "And you know what? That was kind of okay with me.

More and more I was content to stay in with her. When my friends suggested a night out they'd scoff when I told them I was spending *'yet another'* evening with Vivienne. They said I'd aged about ten years in ten weeks." He made a fist, extended his thumb downwards onto the table and pushed his weight down onto it.

"And yes, it's quite likely that was true," signalling his gesture, "but it hardly mattered to me." Alexander spoke frankly, more honestly than Felix could imagine himself speaking should the roles be reversed.

"Call me a hopeless romantic," Alexander spread his hands, "but I was happy to spend all my time with her. I was doing a bit of bar-work at that point, with some painting thrown in here and there – this rich lady used to pay me a tenner an hour to do the groundwork on canvasses she'd later sell for thousands. But painting was painting, so I went along with it." He shrugged. "I always found myself wishing those hours away though, willing the brushstrokes on, knowing that each one was a second closer to seeing her." He stepped out of his story for a minute. "God, when I look back, I feel like some besotted teenager. I suppose that's almost what I was."

"My sense of moderation – not very strong at the best of times –" he broke off and smiled to himself, "– disappeared entirely. I felt completely alive. I felt that what I was doing at that point, with Vivienne, was the right thing, the *only* thing, that I should be doing. And the best thing was, it was all reciprocated. The more of myself I gave to her, the closer we became, until I'd placed practically my whole existence, my whole happiness, in her hands." He sipped. "But boy, was she good with those hands – she never dropped even a crumb. And that's how I lived, alone on the world with her. Those friends who said she had me under her thumb, they stopped calling. The boozy nights in the pubs and in the smoky jazz bars, they all dried up. I didn't even particularly cry to watch them go – I'd found something that transcended all that, something that made all that fall into insignificance. Why would I go out when I had all I wanted in her?"

Felix spoke at last. "You really fell in deep."

"Yes," Alexander nodded. "Yes I did. And then I forced myself further under – tied bricks to my ankles and dived, forever aiming to get deeper. Looking back, I gave up a lot to be with her."

"Isn't that just called growing up?"

"Mmm," Alexander sounded thoughful. "But maybe... maybe I wasn't ready to yet. Maybe I'm still not."

So was that, Felix wondered, how it had all turned sour? Alexander wasn't finished yet.

"I still see some of the friends that I shunned back then. I always feel they don't really know what they're doing with themselves – they keep running, burning their candles at both ends to keep darkness at bay. I sometimes think: what are you running from?"

The look on Felix's face told Alexander he wasn't here for life lessons.

"Anyway," he shook his head, "back to the story. Vivienne worked in a clothes shop. *Couture,* as they call it. She couldn't be seen to be with a scruff – so the scruff had to go, and he was perfectly happy to. For her, anything for her. His shaggy hair was cut, his paint-stained shirts were thrown out. I was suddenly wearing clothes that "actually fitted". Oh, I looked *grand*. I felt a million dollars, especially with Vivienne on my arm. We'd go for drinks in posh bars and laugh and laugh until I damn near fell off my chair. She was a lot of fun," Alexander said. The way he said it sounded like it was the greatest compliment he could pay a woman.

This wasn't really what Felix had come to find out about.

"Okay, so where did it all go wrong?" Felix asked.

"I'm coming to that," said Alexander, holding up his hand.

At that moment a small man with a scarf knotted around his neck approached the table carrying two short, fat glasses containing a colourless liquid. As it wafted up towards Felix, he caught the smell of liquorice. He set one down for Alexander and patted him around the shoulder, muttering a few words into his ear. Alexander answered in one and two-word answers, then said something that made the man hold up his free hand in apology and back off into the crowd. Felix had almost forgotten they were in a room full of people.

Alexander continued, unswayed by the interruption. "When we were together, it was mostly just the two of us. That was the way she preferred it. We had the occasional family gathering, sure, and Vivienne loved those – making sure she looked all prim and proper, making sure that I was neatly presented to your aunts and grannies. It was all about appearance. The front masked any blemishes. Not that there were *any* of those, of course."

It was the first snide thing Alexander had said, and it stung. This woman he spoke harshly of was the woman who'd raised him.

"Nothing was ever wrong. Not on the surface anyway." Alexander breathed a sigh. "But that's hindsight talking. Honestly, I was blind at the time." He picked up his beer and held it in his hand without drinking. "So, we moved in together, and the next logical step was to get married. And then," Alexander said with a smile that Felix didn't reciprocate, "and then you came along."

"So where'd it all go to pieces?"

"She and I were good for so long. She was my everything and could do no wrong. And me? I was a blinkered horse afraid to break contact with those eyes. I see now that I'd taught myself to say but one thing: 'Yes, Vivienne.'"

He'd been animated while talking about the madly-in-love times, but an air of sadness now came over him as the story progressed downhill. He looked around the bar, shuffled in his seat, seemingly seeking something to delay his going on with the story. Uncomfortable as it was for Felix to watch, he pressed on. Alexander had inflicted enough grief upon the family. He could handle having some back.

"Well?"

Alexander knotted his hands together on the table and stared into their core, the darkness in his palms bringing back the blackness of years ago.

"I – " he began, "she – ". He tailed off with a sigh, then tried again. "And it was all fine – I was hers, she was mine. Until suddenly, suddenly something erupted inside Vivienne,

38

some volcano of motherliness. All her tendencies sixfolded – you were the apple of her eye and I was the mismatched third wheel – and suddenly I realised I'd invested so much of myself into her that there was precious little of myself left in me. I was the shell of a man who'd once been capable of living and loving."

Felix had expected the *but*, yet was taken aback to realise it was him.

"Wait," he said incredulously, "*I* was the reason you left?!"

"No, Fe–"

"Cause it's certainly sounding like that," Felix interrupted. As he raised his voice, those nearest them in the bar turned to look at the pair.

"*You* were not the reason I left," Alexander said, his voice controlled but firm. "*I* was. *I* was the reason I was in that mess in the first place – I'd dived too deep and now couldn't breathe. I'd lost my way and my confidence and any sense of direction in my life. In losing her, I'd also lost the enormous part of myself I'd given over to her. I'd given up my friends, my life, painting, all to be with her, and now a tide change occurred. She was no longer mine, she was ours."

Felix was shocked at Alexander's selfishness. "So you couldn't stand sharing her with a child *you* created? A product of you *and* her? Are you deluded?!"

Alexander sat with his head down, like a pupil being reprimanded.

"Should have thought about that *before* you knocked her up. Or was that all her decision too? Did the conversation go: "I want a baby," and you said: "Yes, Vivienne," to keep

39

her happy? Was it ever your wish to bring a child, to bring *me*, into the world?"

"Felix," Alexander said, "we talked about it, we felt ready. And you were a bundle of joy – it was great."

"But clearly not great enough," Felix retorted, finishing the rest of his beer in one go and reaching for his coat. He'd had enough of this shit – he needed space.

"Felix – " Alexander called after him, then got up, excused himself from the artists in a hurry and pushed out onto the street.

Felix didn't know where he was headed as he powered down the dim street, just that he needed to get away from Alexander. But as he strode, the cold air crept into his mind and he realised someone was following him. He'd left to make a statement, but realised he still had questions unanswered. He slowed and let Alexander catch up. They walked in silence for a while, Felix following his view to the Seine, a ribbon of moonlight guiding his way. Alexander now had to play the game as Felix dictated, trying to get his message across and make Felix understand.

"I was so caught," Alexander said. "Between you, and Vivienne, and myself. In the middle of this impossible triangle was a situation where my heart demanded I was true to it, but my brain wasn't able to accept that I had to do this...and," he choked, his voice dropping to a whisper, "*actually* hurt people."

"You *did* hurt us, Alexander," Felix said, stopping and turning to face the man.

"I know."

"No you don't – you buggered off, remember? You *can't* know. The ones who know are me and Mum. We suffered. We had no choice – so *don't* say you know."

Alexander sighed inwardly.

"Okay, I *don't* know. To be honest I don't have a clue what you went through."

"Shall I tell you?!" Felix snapped. "Only years of Mum crying, of her holding on close to me because she was afraid of losing the only other man in her life. Only years of pretending everything was alright at family get-togethers, years of hearing we were doing so well and not believing a word of it because we knew deep down that it was was one giant front we'd put up. *That's* what we went through. Shall I spare you the rest?"

Alexander pursed his lips and looked down at the pavement. Felix shuffled over to a nearby bench and sat down, hands in his coat pockets. Alexander paused for a moment, standing over Felix.

"I'm sorry," he said.

Felix dismissed the statement with a raise of his eyebrows. Alexander sat down carefully next to him, leaving Felix space yet not being too distant. So there they sat in the Parisian night. Father and son, but not really.

"Are you?" Felix asked.

"Yes," said Alexander, "I'm truly sorry for the hurt I caused Vivienne and for the hurt I caused you. You were an innocent victim of my drowning. So too was Vivienne really. I did it to myself, and, in trying to rectify it, in trying to be true to myself, I found the bonds I'd made had got stronger than I could ever imagine – and suddenly it wasn't just about me anymore – suddenly in choosing to do the right thing for myself, I hurt the two people closest to me, probably irreparably."

"And *did* you do the right thing?"

"Y–" Alexander started, then caught himself. "Yes..." he lingered on the word, drawing the final sound out until it sounded like a question. Then he composed himself: "Yes."

Felix was silent. His head swum with the evening's turn of events. It all seemed so irrational. Was Alexander telling him the whole truth? Did the man even really understand it for himself? Not liking the answers, he let the uncomfortable still air sit between them, until it had grown almost physical in its nature.

Alexander broke first.

"Yes," he repeated. "And no."

Felix remained silent.

"Yes, because for once I listened to myself. I'd dissolved myself into Vivienne and completely neglected my friends and my other passions – painting until the early hours, long rambling conversations over drinks. I threw them away when I met Vivienne. Friends stopped calling and my paints dried in their tubes as my existence became more and more purely her. I was an alcoholic in a still, boiling myself away until my love for her was so strong and so intoxicating that it ultimately became self-destructive. So yes, was it the right decision?" Alexander paused for a moment as his voice cracked. He took a deep breath, confronted the word and said: "Yes. It was."

42

"But," he continued, "do I wish the decision could have been taken without hurting you and Vivienne? Yes," he said with the same conviction. "I loathe myself every time I think about it, for letting it run on so far that the only option I saw available was the one I took."

He dropped his head, utterly crestfallen, and spoke into his lap, addressing himself more than anyone else.

"It's one of those things that's such a double-edged sword. Should I have kept more of myself when I fell for Vivienne that hard?" He looked up and squinted out into the night. "Maybe not – but the years I gave her were good. I gave her my absolute *everything* for years," Alexander said, a touch of anger creeping into his voice.

"It sounds like you're trying to convince yourself," Felix spoke his thoughts.

Alexander shrugged. "Every time I think about it I have to reconvince myself – how can a sane mind walk out on a woman he's mad about, who's just carried his son? It doesn't make sense, I *know* that, but..." Alexander paused for thought and breath "but still I *had* to do it. For my own sanity."

"Do you feel sane now?" Felix asked, looking at this mess of a man sitting beside him.

"No – in the way that I don't think artists ever really are. But I'm doing what I love, in a city I love. My life feels good." A pause. "Like I said Felix, hindsight is a beautiful thing. But hindsight also tells me that if I'd chosen not to hurt you and Viv – Vivienne – it would have been a death sentence for my artistic side. Or worse, I'd have had to watch it fester away in solitary confinement."

"Like we did," Felix said. "I can't believe there was *no* reconciliation, no compromise that could be made between your family and '*art*'."

"Please don't belittle it like that. For an artist, the drive to create is strong, stronger sometimes than the urge for sex, sleep, food. It's one of your basic human needs that you'd suffer without. Mentally at first, until that spills over and manifests itself physically. It's something of a beast inside me."

Felix raised one eyebrow, switching off as the conversation approached the conceptual.

"So how did you suppress it for so long with Mum?" he asked.

"Because the beast –"

"Stop with this beast *bullshit*."

Alexander started again. "Because my passion was absorbed with ultimate love for something else – reciprocated love – the kind the artist yearns for. I didn't need a creative outlet when I had her, I didn't need the reassurance of my talent since my talent was in loving her and that was clearly abundant. The appreciation I get for my paintings now, I once got from her and from those around us telling us what a good couple we were. I built my self-esteem out of my projection onto Vivienne. Now I get that from art. When I paint, I put the best version of myself onto the canvas, the very best my brain and hand can create until I'm happy with it, or content at the very least. Then, when I show it to others, there's the pleasure in their appreciation. It's a lot like love when you break it down. Love is a form of art, or art is a form of love, I'm not sure which yet."

Felix was silent again. The conversation had gone off on a tangent, with his question still unanswered. Again: "there was no way of compromise?"

"I tried. Perhaps not as persistently as I should've, but I tried. I tried to involve her in my paintings – hell, I even painted her – but it never really made an impression. And because I valued her opinion so highly, I took that as a sign that it was no good, that *I* was no good. I did the best I could, spent hours trying to reflect her beauty," he paused with an ironic laugh, "*that* in itself was doomed from the very first brushstroke, but it hardly even made a mark. So I turned my back on art as self-expression, as a route to happiness and fulfillment, and turned back to loving her. At least *that* was reciprocated."

"And then you 'lost' her to me, it was reciprocated no longer and suddenly art reared its head again?" Felix summarised.

"Well..." He had nowhere left to go. "Yes Felix, that's exactly right."

Yet still Felix was unconvinced. How could putting paintbrush to canvas make Alexander leave a love of so many years, one that he had produced a child with?

Felix sighed, disgusted. When he started to speak, he only managed a few words, a jumble of sentences before he broke off again.

"I need space," he said eventually.

Alexander nodded but said nothing.

"Just trust me Felix," he said eventually, "I hated having to do it. If there was any way I saw to do it without inflicting what I did on you and Vivienne, I'd have done it. But I just didn't see one."

Felix remained unmoving.

"And I want nothing more than to patch it up with you, no matter how much work that's going to take on my part."

Felix at this point cared for nothing less.

"Let me buy you dinner at least," Alexander's voice was almost pleading.

Felix sat silently.

"I'll give you my number. Call me if you feel up for it."

Still no word. After a minute, Felix slid out his phone, took down Alexander's number, then buttoned up his coat and walked off into the night without a word. He didn't look back, but if he had, he'd have seen Alexander still sitting there. In fact, if he'd returned an hour later, he'd still have found Alexander there, caught on the high wire of his decision.

Felix walked the full five kilometres back to the hotel. His legs were on autopilot, guided at times by the shining Sacré-Cœur like a jewel over the city. He walked with but one thought in his mind, crossing dark roads and turning corners without even noticing. One sole thought: "How can art win over love?" It echoed in his mind, the steps he hardly realised he took drumming the beat of the words into his head: "How can *art*, win over *love*?"

An hour later, he was back at the hotel, still no nearer an answer, no nearer understanding. Unlocking the door to his room, he crossed to the windows and pulled them open. Outside, a small ledge of concrete jutted out, with cast-iron work looping and soaring from it, forming patterns that whorled and swum in front of his weary eyes. He put a foot up on the ledge and looked out into the night. A glow hung over the city, staining the clouds with a murky glow and obscuring any stars. His hands on the railings, he cursed Alexander under his breath. Finding the metal loose, he rattled the railing, crashing iron into concrete. He cursed down the street, out loud this time, scolding his *stupid* decision to pursue this brazen dream in a city where there was someone he'd once shared his life with, but not a soul he really knew.

"What will become of me?" he wondered, leaning his head on the railing until his vision became a dull sea of grey and black. Should he leave? He imagined the bus-ride home, twelve hours cooped up in his head with only his failure and his anger for company. He imagined his mother's smug grin, her silent "*I told you so*".

No.

When it came down to it, leaving now only left him with more unfinished business. He pulled the curtains over the window and lay down on his bed, staring at the dark ceiling.

*

He was at a restaurant with Vivienne and Alexander. The venue had clearly been chosen by his mother. The neat white tablecloths, discrete waiters and little abstract sculptures on the tables gave that away. The wine glasses stood, waiting to be filled, refracting light falling in through the large windows and sending rainbows across the table. The fact the three of them sat at a single table didn't even occur to Felix as strange. The pair chatted amicably, animatedly even, Alexander's hand curled around Vivienne's as it sat on the table. Felix leaned closer. They were definitely communicating – Alexander laughing at something Vivienne said, Vivienne then nodding at Alexander's story – but to Felix's ear they spoke distinctly separate languages. He looked around; was he the only one hearing this? How were they communicating so seemingly flawlessly despite being worlds apart in what they spoke?

Felix woke and stretched, perplexed by the fading dream. He couldn't yet face the prospect of talking to Alexander again, so got dressed and headed out onto the streets. The air had taken on a freshness as the day hung poised in its starting blocks. Ornate sandstone buildings rose up on all sides, with cast iron railings shielding balconies and white shutters guarding the windows. Felix peered into what he could see of other people's houses and into other people's lives. Some, impenetrable, had their shutters closed. Much like some people, Felix thought. The sun glinted off the steep slate attic roofs. The one touch of colour in the street was the rolled up red awnings of another hotel, flapping in the breeze.

He walked on, approaching Montmartre. As he climbed the first set of stairs to the flat concrete base of the hill, a café was opening up. At the *Café au Jardins* a girl was moving the last of the chairs into position around the brushed metal tables. A small child ran happily after the pigeons. A grubby bearded man sat, cradling a dog in his arms, with his back to the base of the enormous staircase leading up to the basilica. Besides them, the area was deserted. Felix made his way over to the café and pulled back a chair, which grated horribly on the concrete. A few wisps of cloud hung in the air, looking like the remnants of a snuffed candle. A lazy plane drifted overhead.

The waitress turned at the sound and looked up at Felix. Her dark hair fell around her shoulders, clad in a plain white t-shirt with a black apron tied around her waist. Her bare arms had a glorious Mediterranean hue. She wiped down a last table and came over, pulling a pen and notepad from the waistband of her apron.

"*Bonjour*," she said cheerily.

"Hello," Felix replied.

"Can I take your *commande*?"

Felix found himself smiling and ordering breakfast. The waitress smiled back, tucked her pen and notepad away and walked off. A minute later she was back, holding a steaming cup and a croissant. Her brown eyes met his.

"Enjoy." She was still smiling as she turned to go, her eyes lingering a second too long on his.

Things were good, Felix decided, as he sipped his hot coffee and reveled in the good weather. The world was blowing out his cobwebs and the morning cloud in his head were nowhere to be found. He polished off the croissant as the waitress stood in the doorway, leaning against the doorframe looking out. She wandered over to rearrange chairs that didn't need rearranging.

"Care to join?" Felix asked.

"I am *weurking*," the girl said.

"So you would if you weren't?"

"*Pardon*?"

"Are you from around here?"

She stopped shifting chairs and came over.

"I am from *ze sauws* of France, but I live here now six years," she said. "And you?"

"I'm here for a visit," Felix said, without going into further detail.

"Ah, a *touriste*." She smiled playfully. "Where do you go today, the Eiffel Tower?"

Felix raised an eyebrow.

Her name, he found out, was Senna, and Felix nodded at the exotic ring it had to it.

"Well, Senna," he said, "I'm sure they haven't got you working all day *and* all night, so what do you say we meet for a drink this evening?"

The slight pause that followed made him stumble slightly in his brain. Had he been too forward with this girl he'd only just met?

"Uhm, okay," Senna said, shrugging slightly. Perhaps he had been, but it had paid off now.

As he paid, he wrote his number on the back of the bill and handed it back, number side up.

"See you later," he said, strolling off. Funny, he thought.

50

We're all keeping up a façade of civilised society and social norms, when really all we are is just glorified chimps. The real life goes on backstage.

It had worked, but did he have any real guarantee that she'd pick up her phone, dial his digits and press *call*? If not, he reassured himself, he'd probably never see her again. She'd fade back into the mass of seven billion people she'd emerged from half an hour before.

At Abesses, Felix dived into the métro. Tunnels roared by, doors wheezed open and shut, passengers came and went. He changed train at St-Lazare, eventually leaving the train at Châtelet.

He traipsed up the steps, through the gates and emerged onto the street. Momentarily disorientated, he could only see more apartment blocks. The glorious cathedral he was looking for was nowhere to be seen. Then he spotted a sign, turned the corner and looked across the bridge at what he had come to see. Paris opened up into a wide sky, bringing with it a first pang of guilt. *Had* he been the reason Alexander had left? Did Vivienne know this? She'd certainly never mentioned anything to Felix and had certainly never acted in that way towards him. But did she know *anything* much about the whole situation?

As he crossed the Pont au Change, he looked down to where a boat passed by on the waves of the river, packed on both decks with tourists. He arrived not long after at the island, sitting proudly in the heart of the Seine, and made his way to Notre-Dame. It loomed large over the nearby rooftops, three resplendent carved doors becoming two imposing towers, an enormous stained-glass roundel at its heart. The entire façade was a work of art, adorned with countless angels, curving arches and looping carvings.

The square was aflurry with activity. As Felix sat on a stone bench facing the cathedral, tourists and tour groups milled around, umbrellas raised by guides desperate to keep their groups together. A garishly-clothed woman stood absorbed behind her easel, painting the crowds and the early-afternoon light on the church. A few more attempted to lure members of the crowd to have their portraits drawn as a souvenir. As Felix sat, the bells rang out, then tolled twice, echoing across the river on both sides.

Would she call?

Tourists moseyed in and out of the cathedral in ones and twos. Felix sat back and soaked up the scene. It really was a breathtaking piece of architecture, he thought, remarkable in its size and awe-inspiring in its design.

Would he call Alexander? He can wait, thought Felix.

He realised now a gap in his own understanding of what had happened all those years ago. Vivienne only ever made reference to it as a timestamp, a landmark in time used to describe when something took place, minimising the meaning it carried with it. Had they fought? Had he at least tried to make Vivienne understand? Felix had been only 5 at the time and remembered little of the specifics, to the extent that in his mind, the conceptual had taken precedence over the practical.

He started walking across the bridge to the opposite side

of the river. The banks here were divided into two levels; one beside the river was pedestrian terrain; the other, high-up and tree lined, those on foot had to share with cars. He strolled the upper level of the Rive Gauche, taking in the rows of painted book stands on the wall, adorned with row upon row of tomes. He paused to flick through a few books. Most were in French, but there were a few in German and even one or two in English. Each stand seemed to have its speciality: science fiction from the 1970s, historical books, leather-bound classics. Their impression of having seen the world, some of them several times over was what drew Felix to them, a quaint memory of history showcased on the banks of this city. Some stalls sold canvases of Parisian scenes, others hawked miniature Eiffel towers, 3 for €1. Sullen men sat nearby, smoking cigarettes, keeping watch over the books. The magic of it was clearly lost on them.

Felix paused at the restaurants on the street, reading each menu in turn. He chose a place serving mussels and sat down for a pint and a steaming pot of seafood, delivered, like any meal worth eating in this city, with a basket of fresh baguette. This was one of Vivienne's favourites, eaten straight from the pot in a rare diversion from her polite, sensible norms. He only knew how hard the whole thing had been for her by accident – the times he'd come home from school to find her in tears or the overheard conversations with older members of the family. Implicitly though, it had affected her behaviour towards him, no doubt. She was more wary, more cautious. She'd taken his leaving for university with a brave face, but Felix now realised it must have dredged up a whole barrel of suppressed memories. On the other hand, to hold back from doing it so as not to hurt his mother would just prolong the legacy – as would not going on this trip – wouldn't it? With some effort, he justified his position to himself. Sometimes the past had to be confronted.

When he'd finished lunch, he paid and headed back towards the hotel. As he left the train at Pigalle, he ventured up the hill to see Montmartre in the daytime. By day, the crest of the hill attracted a more traditional visitor. As Felix did his best to get round Place de Tertre, a whole host of artists were selling paintings of the city – some sombre street scenes, others brightly-coloured abstracts. Portrait painters called out to Felix hopefully. The cafés in the middle of the square were heaving, dappled by the sun coming through the trees. His phone itched in his pocket.

He returned to the hotel around 5, with still not a cloud visible in the slowly bruising sky. He lay on his bed and picked up his book. Two pages in, he realised he was reading without taking in. He gave up and put the book aside. Though he'd kept time free in the hope that Senna would call, he couldn't wait all night. The evening lay empty ahead of him. Should he call Alexander? Could he face the man a second time in as many days? His only alternative, he realised, was to lie in bed all evening until it got late enough to sleep. That certainly wouldn't help.

He picked up his phone. Alexander was at the top of his contacts list. Unconvinced of his actions, Felix found himself dialling the number, half-hoping there would be no answer. Four rings in he heard his own voice, aged, back down the line. It was like listening to a voice transformer.

"*Allo*?" 52-year-old Felix inquired.

"It's Felix."

"Ah, Felix," Alexander perked up.

"Dinner?"

"Absolutely. What time suits?"

"Let's say 7:30."

"Right – I know a little place that will be busy. I'll meet you on Rue Damremont at 7:30."

"Okay, see you there."

Felix hung up.

He must've drifted off, for the next thing Felix knew, his room was dark. He checked the time. *18:30*. Perfect. He showered and got dressed, pulling on a jacket over a white shirt. His dark jeans and shoes fell on the right side of smart-casual. He left the hotel at 7. Still no word from Senna – was that it?

It was a twenty minute walk to Rue Damremont. As he walked, he felt yesterday's anger rising in him again. He clenched his fists, then exhaled and let his hands drop by his sides.

He arrived early at Rue Damremont. The road was long and curved around beyond his line of sight. Had they agreed a place to meet? Felix walked up the road, crossed at the top and walked back. He found a bench and sat down. Was he going to be stood up again? The temperature wasn't far off single-figures and Felix hadn't really prepared for the cold. The open collar of his shirt let in the breeze and his toes grew numb through his shoes. After a few minutes he got up and walked to the nearest bar, *Jules Verne* emblazoned on the green awnings. He pulled a stool up to the bar, ordered a beer and waited. It was only as he took his first sip from his *demi* – the glass cold on his fingers, the liquid icy on his throat – that he realised how thirsty he was.

Felix was in the bar for a good half hour before his phone buzzed in his pocket. He grasped for it urgently – would it be...? – wrestled it out and turned the screen to face him.

"Alexander" flashed up on the screen. Oh well.

"Hello?" Felix said, annoyance in his voice.

"I'm here," he made no mention of being late. "Are you around?"

"Yeah, come to *Jules Verne*."

"Give me a minute."

A minute became several, and it was a good ten minutes before Alexander eventually entered the bar. He nodded at Felix and pulled a smile across his face. Felix was further irked by Alexander's tardiness and apparent lack of remorse. He nodded at Alexander, who pulled over a bar stool and lifted himself up into it. Catching the barman's eye and seeing Felix's near-empty second glass, he ordered two more. Felix hadn't eaten since the mussels that afternoon and was starting to feel it going to his head. He finished the lukewarm remains as two fresh *demis* were placed on the bar in front of them. Alexander tried to set the tone with smalltalk.

"Been up to much today?" he asked.

"Not really, went to Notre Dame," he replied.

"Ah, beautiful," Alexander said.

"It was good."

"Good? It's astonishing. Beauty beyond anything else in this city."

"Mmm," Felix concurred. "You?"

"Me?" Alexander seemed absent-minded.

"Do much today?"

"Oh – not really. I only got to bed around three."

"Ah," Felix said. Had Alexander gone off somewhere last night? That trivialised matters.

"I started on a new piece. It's meant to be going in an exhibition at some fair soon."

"I didn't know you were that good," Felix said.

"Good –" Alexander frowned, "what's good? No Felix, what you need to know is what's in fashion, what the people want to see."

"That's a very corporate way of looking at it," Felix said.

"It's a very contemporary way of looking at it," Alexander said. "And judging by proceedings so far, it's quite a lucrative way of looking at it."

"It's not very artistic though, is it?" Felix couldn't resist a stir.

"Not a lot in the art world is, I'm afraid. I've come to discover a world of nepotism, inflated values and arse-licking for listing in this or that directory, or for a piece in this or that exhibition. Money's ruined a lot for art. People see expensive paintings as good paintings, but all a six-figure price tag indicates is a good investment." Alexander sat back on this thought.

Felix asked, "What is it you're painting?"

"It's a complex piece, I'm really challenging myself with it. In short, it's a still life set out on a velvet cloth. But it's got a painting in it too, so essentially it's two paintings in one – and that's not mentioning the folds and the sheen of the velvet."

"Will it be for sale?" Felix asked.

Alexander gave a dry smile. "Yes, I'm looking for about ten grand considering the work that'll go into it."

"Is that a lot?" Felix asked.

"Not compared to the Rothko's of this world, but what use is money when you're dead? It's a reasonable amount, and it'll pay the bills for a while, but it's not often I could do something like this. Most go for less. And then the gallery takes a cut –" here he interrupted himself. "Well, less a cut, more a gaping gash. But hey, we rely on them, so what can we do?"

Felix recognised disillusion in Alexander's voice. All he'd done since he got here was a sorrowful attack on the thing he'd supposedly left Vivienne and Felix for, fifteen years ago.

"Sounds a great world to be in. Definitely worth leaving a wife and son for."

Alexander looked hurt. "I didn't –" he stumbled, almost not wanting to utter the next words. "I didn't leave to join the art world. I left to pursue my dream of being a painter. I left because the suppressed love for painting haunted me, and only came back stronger when I tried to contain it. I couldn't feed both that beast and satisfy your mother. Something had to give."

"Yes," Felix said, "and that something was us. We sure gave. *Gave* our everything to keep up a front of normalcy when inside, Mum was a wreck. We still gave a shit – years after we should have decided we wouldn't anymore."

"Yes, Felix, I kn–" he stopped short. "I realise that I put you through some very tough times," he picked his words carefully. "And I've explained my reasons for that as best I can."

"And yet it's still not clear how you chose for painting over a woman you loved and a child you'd created. It's beyond selfish, Alexander, that's what it is."

"Ultimately, that's all it is." Alexander said, catching Felix off-guard. "It was a wildly selfish decision. I chose for myself at the expense of two people to whom I was everything."

"I don't see how an inanimate floaty concept can win over a flesh-and-blood attractive lady. How can this 'art' be so important to you?"

Alexander sat for a moment, thinking out his answer. "I don't know. I'm still not sure if it's something you have from birth or whether it's something picked up along the road of life. But it's present in everything – I've found artists are on the whole much more perceptive people. They'll notice things others just pass without a glance. They're a certain kind of person, Felix, it's nigh on written in their fate. And so I find somewhere inside me an artist living, influencing my every move. I couldn't ignore it. The urge to create grew too strong, too all-encompassing to set it to one side as a folly. It was my best friend and my worst enemy at the same time – a drug that left me exhilarated and wanting – and eventually needing – more."

So Alexander had given up on them for an addiction.

That felt good. Felix still couldn't muster this incredible piece of supposed fact.

Part of his mind, he admitted to himself, was thinking about Vivienne and what he'd tell her when he went home. If she asked anything about the trip at all – and she was prone to skirt the awkward conversation entirely, as if by not discussing it, it would became less real – she would require a good explanation of a situation she couldn't begin to comprehend. Only then would it go some way to providing closure for Vivienne. Felix wondered, though, if he'd ever get his own head around it.

They ate later in a bustling hive of activity, an Italian full of loud locals. Maps of Italy and tall jars of dry pasta lined the walls as waiters hurried by in immaculate white shirts carrying steaming bowls of pasta and large pizzas. Alexander greeted the waiter like a close friend.

"Regular haunt?" Felix asked, after Alexander had finished his conversation with the waiter about who was in, who was out, and who was in and out of whom.

"I've been here before, yes." Alexander said.

Felix ate ravenously, making up for his early lunch and espresso breakfast. Conversation was wooden over dinner. Felix busied himself with his food so as to fend off any of Alexander's attempts at smalltalk.

It was a narrow restaurant, and it was often a squeeze to let waiters and punters past the table. Alexander cut up his pizza and ate it with his hands, one elbow resting on the table. He looked ill at ease with the uneasy silence; caught between wanting to forge a bond with this young man, yet all the while understanding Felix need for space to deal with things in his own time.

Felix's phone buzzed in his pocket. He reached for it instinctively, hopefully, ignoring restaurant etiquette. Senna. A full twelve hours after he'd met – 'met' – her, she'd delivered the goods. Felix smiled into his phone.

"*Sorry ;)*" she'd typed.

Felix was thrown. So that was a no, at least for tonight. But it wasn't quite a no forever. She'd made the bold move of allowing him her number; that in itself was more important than the content of the message. And a wink?

He put his phone away.

When the bill came, Alexander put down a few notes from his battered wallet. Felix nodded by means of a thank-you. As they left, Alexander pressed a coin into the waiter's hand.

"I know somewhere nearby, if you're up for another drink," Alexander offered hopefully.

"Sure," Felix said. They'd had a bottle of wine over dinner and he was feeling both that and the beers from *Jules Verne*.

"Great," Alexander sounded pleasantly surprised. As they passed a *Tabac*, he motioned to Felix to wait, then darted inside. As Felix waited, a black and white cat crossed the street ahead of him. Felix watched it strut for a few paces, then freeze, caught in the headlights of an approaching car. He saw the glare reflected back in its terrified eyes, as it stood rooted to the spot, unsure of what to do in the face of this incoming giant. A second later it was gone, hidden under the body of a much safer parked car.

Alexander came out a few moments later, holding a bottle of red wine in his hand. He held it up to Felix, seeking approval.

"You like red?"

"Bit late now if I don't," Felix said. Alexander's question was left hanging without an answer.

They cut down a side-street, dimly lit and smelling of overflowing bin bags and urine. Another turn and they'd reached the Seine. They heard the river before they reached it, courtesy of a celebration of noise creeping up the walls from the bank.

"Down here?" Felix asked.

Alexander nodded and pushed ahead as they picked their way down the steps, clambering past students of all origins and French people of all ages, towards a wall of sound storming up at them from a group of about ten musicians. This was clearly a meeting spot. Most sitting down were armed with cans of cheap lager or bottles of wine.

They made their way to the wall of the river, the water lapping not far below where they sat. Beside them perched a homeless man, a dog curled up at his feet, gnawing at an unopened bottle of water and bits of baguette the man occasionally fed him. Eventually, as the dog sunk his teeth deep into it, the bottle burst, and the dog pressed its paw down upon it and lapped the water as it shot towards him. The music climbed the steep wall between them and the road, crept into the gaps in the cobblestones and was reflected on the happy faces, numbering a hundred or more. Felix found his mood lifting with the music. Alexander cracked the bottle open and they sat in silence, yet far from silence, drinking in the atmosphere and the wine. Felix was glad for some distraction masking the silence between the two. The music continued relentlessly, as Felix drank from the bottle almost without realising. The saxophone rasped over the top, blowing a solo into the year's early air while the double bass tones sat fat like a bullfrog in the background. All members of the band stood, even the drummer, choosing to hang his scaled-down set from his neck as if in a marching band. A flute player who Felix had hardly noticed piped up with a solo of springtime birdsong that sounded like it came from the very trees above them. Felix found himself drifting on the music, carried along on the wine biting his lips, but inside felt warm and at ease. He rose up on the synchronicity of the music, the perfect balance of sounds and the swaggering style with which they played. Each musician grooved their own part, both musically and physically, moving and swaying to the sounds plucked from the air – part rehearsed, part purely felt. When the piece receded into silence, Felix found himself applauding, back in the real world and surrounded by real people. He felt the cold stone hard beneath him and blinked as if awaking from slumber, recognising the feeling of being away but never having experienced it through music before. He turned to Alexander with a smile of amazement on his face – quite forgetting for a moment that he was supposed to be angry at him. For a moment he felt free, high above the night in a world of his own. He suddenly felt a unity in his mind, with who he was and with what he was doing. Any doubt had evaporated from the warmth of the music and had dispersed into the cloudless night.

The applause faded away and the band's harmonica player, the ringleader of the pack, announced the next song, entitled: "Oh, what it is to be by the Seine." How fitting, Felix thought. It was a slow soulful song, telling of couples strolling by the river hand in hand. Though Felix walked amongst them with a girl by his side, he only caught glimpses of her face as streetlights lit their way.

"Oh, what it is to be by the Seine – with you," the song concluded, sweeping Felix back into the real world of Paris. He was surprised at the strength of the musical current as it pulled him and lifted him away from the city into a place of quasi-dreams, not told where to go but following the music up inside his brain – not directed but following notes instinctively to new places, new thoughts, new feelings he'd never experienced before. It was as if the music had rubbed off his shell of apathy, dispelled the clouds in his brain and enabled him to be a man, to be full of energy and passion and to live life not locked up behind the walls of his mind. He remembered this feeling from his night at the Sacré-Cœur, the full impact of his thoughts almighty – but that's all they were, just thoughts, just feelings that dried up overnight and left him in a ditch in the morning. If only he could do something with them – if only he could hold them tight in this state and not lose them after a few hours of sleep. If he could do that, he could do anything.

Felix was a million miles away, and initially did not hear Alexander talking.

"There's often music down here," he said. "Warming up the banks of the Seine in the winter and keeping them icy-cold in summer."

"I was miles away," Felix said as he gasped for breath.

"That's the idea of art," Alexander said, knowingly.

Felix could scarcely believe his mental journey.

"But –" he started, "I was *living*, high above the world, in a world like ours but much more beautiful, like some parallel universe, and," he continued, "and everything was beautiful. It was like the world was warmed up – colours brighter, people friendlier, everything more raw."

Alexander couldn't help but smile a smile of nostalgia. They sat in silence a little longer, basking in the applause clattering off the walls like hailstones. As the next song came around, a tourist boat, the kind Felix had seen that afternoon, growled into view on the river. Stacked to the rafters again with tourists, at night these boats were armed with lights that would make many a construction site proud, lighting up the banks of the Seine, giving the tourists on board the impression they were actually seeing something – without realising of course that what these tourists came to see was the night-light, street-light views of Paris. But then, Felix thought, people often did strange things in the name of money.

As the boat passed by, these lights fell over the scene, engulfing the musicians and the punters in a harsh glow. As Felix watched, the motley collection of the homeless man, the local, the tourist and the musician were scattered onto the walls of the Seine – a silhouette portrait in which everyone's shadow was simultaneously everyone else's, no man and Everyman at the same time. The scene blurred lines between the known and the unknown, the friend and the stranger, bonding all stories into a storybook tableau that Felix could not draw his eyes away from. The tuba player became a cobra, his head writhing in time with the music and spitting jazz over the river where it floated lazily on the breeze and settled on the tide; the sax became a dancing bear, breaking from daytime captivity to sing a song of freedom. The double-bassist became even more one with his instrument, holding it as he would a dance partner but thumping it with incredible vigour. As heads bobbed in black and brick, Felix knew it was the most beautiful thing he had ever seen. While the vision combined with the music as part of the show – sporadic, absurd and free – Felix imagined himself on the boat, harbouring a longing to join the folk on the bank, to linger and hear the full richness of the music over the drone of the engines. Now though, he realised, he was free to remain sitting, wine bottle in hand and frequently at his lips, drinking in the scene for as long as it lasted. And it would end, as everything in this world did. As sure as the passing of seasons, at some point during the evening the musicians would pack away their instruments, their magical sound machines and up and go, to their beds – or someone else's. He'd be left, dropped back into the real world, confronted by the fact that he was now again sitting next to Alexander, a man who had caused his mother such pain.

The band played a song accompanied by an accordion, eastern European in its sound. Judging by some of the musicians, it was probably the sort of music they'd grown up with. It transported Felix to the feeling of a festival: long days of rising as the sun broke into the tent and burned them out into the air, still groggy from the night before and blinking at the harsh daylight. As he emerged from the tent, a few people sat on canvas chairs outside their tents nursing hangovers and mugs of coffee. Somewhere in the background, the accordion fell away and a guitar picked up – somewhere in front of a nearby tent someone was playing early morning chords to the world. He imagined long days of lazy grass lounging, of beers and of falling in and out of valleys of sun-touched sleep. Later, there would be impromptu campfires, long improvised sessions as dreadlocks drummed rhythms on cool-boxes, as harmonicas produced from back pockets of worn jeans drew the night's stragglers together.

The waves of music had entered him and would not let him go. The gathering's glory lay in the stumbling upon this spontaneous gig by the river, the lack of expectation, the fact that a coincidence of coordinates brought these people together physically but also very much psychologically – as if by being here, these people qualified themselves as good people, free people, without their exchanging a word. Felix knew he liked these folk just for their being here. It was a feeling that would only be diluted if these guys made it big, if they stopped playing by the Seine and lived the lives of millionaires behind tinted glass and shielded by bodyguards. It was their accessibility, the fact Felix could literally go up and touch them, the fact he was this close to this much genius that so few people knew about that made them so impressive.

Imagine these guys made music their living. Imagine they sold albums and sold out arenas. Would there then be any art left in their performance?

From somewhere far away, Felix heard shouting. He jerked back into the world and saw torch-beams circling on the ground, this time not from a boat, but from the road high above. Three heads poked over the parapet, adorned with flat blue caps. The band kept playing, until the men above identified the ringleader and shone their torches in his face. Loving the attention, the man continued to dance and jive, the crowd applauding and whooping wildly, loving the show. The men above couldn't be heard over the jubilation of the crowd. They started picking a slow path down the steps, out of their comfort zone on high, clambering over bodies, bags and hastily-concealed bottles. It emerged that the three were police officers, directed to break up a noisy rebellion on the banks of the Seine – where they were causing no problems, contained in a happy little bubble – for the sake of Parisian peace. Some rich folk had probably complained of the noise ruining their sleep and the value of their property. The police spoke to the ringleader who danced on as the band kept playing behind him, oblivious to the boys in blue. The ringleader held up five fingers, one for each of the minutes he planned to continue playing. The men relented. The ringleader extended his arm into the night, keeping his five fingers aloft in victory to a chorus of cheers, as the men retreated back up the stairs.

Ten minutes of music later they were back, more annoyed this time, and the ringleader signalled to the band to wind down. Leisurely, the saxophonist finished his raspy midnight solo, and one by one the musicians played quieter and and quieter and then fell still, to a chorus of jeers and boos from the crowd. When the police retreated again and the musicians started packing away their instruments, a roar of appreciation at the musicians and outrage at the police started in one corner of the audience, quickly spreading until the whole crowd were on their feet, Felix included, cheering and applauding these mysterious men who had defied convention and law to bring them a show. Fans flocked around the band who stood breathless but modest at the centre of their own celebration. What had probably started as a rehearsal had turned into a hundred-strong baying crowd, hungry for more. Felix headed over to the drummer who was unscrewing his drums from his holster.

Felix raved, "That was amazing – thank you."

The man remained modest, thanking Felix for his praise and saying something derogatory through a thick French accent about the police.

"Do you play here often?" Felix asked, mainly to remain briefly in the presence of genius.

"We play everywhere," the man said with a laugh.

Felix thanked the man again and went over to the hat they'd put down, already spilling over with coins and notes. Dipping into his wallet, he found only a €10 note. He thought about it briefly and then dropped it into the hat, winking at the ringleader as he rose up again. The man clasped his hands together, bowing slightly as he called a "*Merci!*" after him. Felix sauntered back to Alexander, yesterday's anger forgotten. Here now sat a man who'd shared his experience, a man who knew exactly – well, maybe not exactly, but nearly – what it meant to be here: the spontaneity, the absurdity, the freedom of having been at just the right place at just the right time to catch this show of which not a trace would exist in the morning, save the crowd's collective memory. Alexander held out the bottle to Felix, the last sip still in the bottom. And then a strange thing happened. Taking the bottle in his left hand, he clapped his right onto Alexander's still-outstretched arm, as he would with a long-lost friend. Felix pulled away after a second. Both men were slightly taken aback, but it had been long enough to plant a seed in both mens' heads.

As the rabble of the excited crowd died down, Felix led the way back up the stairs after passing the tuba player with a slap on the shoulder and a smile. Who was this man who Felix felt himself being?

"Have you been to the Louvre?" Alexander asked as they were about to part ways at the top.

"No, worth doing?" Felix asked, with one eye on what to do tomorrow and on whether to suggest to Alexander to meet up again.

"Most worth-doing thing there is in Paris. Want to go?"

"Sure," Felix found himself saying, not wholly dissatisfied with his instinctive answer.

"I can't make tomorrow, but let's say Friday. Meet me out front, by the glass pyramid, at two."

"Okay," Felix agreed.

"Bring good hiking boots," joked Alexander. "It's massive.

A compass would be good too, if you've got one."

Felix said he'd look for one, then forgot all about it.

They parted ways.

Lying on his bed he pulled out his phone, remembering Senna. The clock blinked 01:34 at him. Too late to text back? Would she think he'd been out boozing? Well, he had been. And this was who he was. He squinted at his screen to force his eyes to focus and typed: "7pm in the Café des Touristes, Montmartre." He read it back – no, too forward. Besides, maybe she'd be working.

"*Free tomorrow for a drink?*" He looked at it again, put an x at the end and hit send. It'd have to do. He stripped off and dived into bed.

*

He awoke as his phone beeped next to his face. Senna. God, her shifts started early. "*Les Grandes Dames on Rue Alphonse. I'll be there from ten with friends x*" He read the text aloud in a French accent. She clearly didn't have an early start the next day.

Unlike recent hangovers, Felix felt good in himself. This hangover, he decided, would be graceful – no psychological car-crash to take into the day, no black streets of time to kill. He was a free, single man in Paris and was eager to show the world what he was made of.

An alarm he didn't even remember setting went off for 10am, and far-off church bells drifted in through his open window. His room was still a mess but it could remain so. Each day the cleaner attempted to create some order, pulling the sheets tight and straightening the pillows, but it felt like a resigned attempt at window-dressing a particularly shabby shop.

He made a point of not breakfasting at the same café to preserve the mutual mystery that was driving this pursuit along. Senna could be anyone. The realm of possibility lay open as Felix was transported back to being a child seeing a present still wrapped under the tree on Christmas Day. He knew he wanted whatever was inside, but exactly what it was remained wholly unknown. Except to Senna, who had lived for years – 21 at a guess – knowing exactly what was inside the wrapping. Or maybe she didn't. Just as Felix was now discovering new facets of himself when thrown into new situations, so too perhaps was she. So too perhaps – probably – was everyone, a life of learning who this body and mind were that they'd been placed into. Or maybe people didn't give it a second thought.

After breakfast, he took to wandering the roads of Montparnasse. An empty can rolled along the cobbles of Rue Servandoni, caught by each gust of wind as if kicked. Winding cobblestone streets curled around. Where each road went he couldn't see beyond their gentle bends. The area was empty – most people chained behind desks at this hour. As he walked, he caught the sound of laughter running down the streets, of church bells from some indeterminable church, of springtime sparrows chirping in newly-blossoming trees. Why couldn't the English build cities like this anymore? Why did cities now have to be contests as to who could build highest, drive fastest, dig deepest? We've lost the romanticism of cities as places for people to meet, of places for couples to stroll, Felix thought. All they had over the Channel was faceless developments full of rushing commuters and crashing computers. How anyone met anyone else in those environments was a mystery – a victory of humanity over capitalism.

Felix walked on, alone. He stumbled across a courtyard, accessible only on foot. At one end stood an unassuming church. The rest of the square was flanked by houses, their windows opening out onto the quiet stones. A few tourists stood snapping shots of the fountain at its centre which filled the square with its trickling whisper. A small child in a miniature France football shirt, unwieldy in his coordination, stumbled as he kicked a ball back to his father. A couple emerged from the church. Following them out from inside came a man out who slotted a heavy padlock into place over the entrance. Felix walked over to the steps of the church and sat down. The angry mob on his brain had moved off for now and left him with a serene emptiness – not the cotton wool he'd known of late but a freshness of soul. The square was now still. He sat for a minute of calm, with nowhere to be, no buzzing phone, not a single obligation. As Felix's thoughts took hold, he imagined the well-to-do French couples that called the square home. He watched them in his mind's eye as they exited the front door, he in loafers, a dapper jacket and a scarf, she in heels with legs that went on forever. The imaginary couple didn't notice him as they walked past arm in arm, then took a right and left the four-walled haven. Eventually, Felix levered himself up and crossed the square to the main door he'd seen being locked. Beside it, he spotted a smaller door in the wall. Something in his brain told him to try the handle. It was a big metal affair, cold to the touch, but when he pushed it down it clicked and swung inwards ajar. Felix stepped over the threshold and closed the heavy wooden door behind him. In the entry hall, he was momentarily plunged into pitch-black, until his eyes adjusted to the gloom and he could see light illuminating the brickwork a few paces from him. Rounding a corner, he found himself at the fork of two paths, going off at right-angles to each other, with a square garden at their heart. The church cloister – of course. In an already calm square, this was a further haven of peace, nestled behind bricks and unseen by most eyes going about their daily lives. He dared not tread on the garden paths, and instead decided to walk the square of pathways surrounding them, segregated by a brick wall about the height of his waist. As he made his way along one wall, he heard women's voices far off, as if coming to him in a dream. On the outside wall, doors led off to rooms and lives up above, but Felix didn't venture up. That, he felt, would be intruding a step too far. The garden at the centre was divided up into four beds with narrow pathways crossing them at right angles. Clearly battling to come back to life after the winter, buds were already appearing on the bushes. A dried-up basin stood on a pedestal at the heart of the garden. Two chairs had been left out, and Felix imagined two old men sitting for long afternoons. He imagined walking these four paths with a girl beside him, saw in his mind's eye how they'd lapse into a silence of understanding for the peace of this place, an understanding of each others' awe and admiration of the place as they paused only to brush hands as a sign of continued presence by each other's side and in each other's thoughts.

Felix snapped back to empty reality on hearing laughter. He felt now as if he were the last person left alive, left behind with the ghosts of those who had gone before. He arrived back at the entrance on the fourth side of this board game, paused briefly, looking back, then pushed the handle down to let himself out. As he did, he heard a bustle from the square as a rowdy school group stormed through.

Felix ducked back into the cloister, unwilling to let the group destroy the serenity of the place. When they'd gone, he ventured back out onto the square, like a hedgehog emerging from the hedgerow.

*

It had been almost dark when he lay down, but his room was now solely lit by the glow from the street below, the light echoing up into his room. Outside, the road was quiet. It was 9:30 and he felt groggy from having slept for too long. His first thought was to go straight back to sleep, but he couldn't let Senna down and still expect to see her. She'd already gained more importance in his mind than their quick conversation at the café merited and Felix felt somehow invested in the chase now.

He got up and went to take a shower, then stood in front of the steamed-up mirror doing his hair and brushing his teeth. He'd been in the city longer than he'd expected and he was running out of clean clothes to wear. He found a shirt, pulled it on and tried to smooth over the creases. It wouldn't do to turn up at 10 on the dot, so Felix walked down to the reception to ask for a *fer-a-repasser*, which they brought to his room. That was better, he thought, eyeing himself in the mirror. Sharp.

Around 10:30 he made it to the bar on Rue Alphonse. It was full of people of his age, and for a moment he was concerned that he wouldn't be able to find Senna. He pushed through the crowds in the bar, scanning faces left and right. He recognised not a soul. Should he get a drink? Then, at the back of the bar, he found her sitting at a round table. In that second, he remembered exactly why he had been so interested before. He put a hand on her shoulder, and she turned and looked up at him with a smile. Felix got a chair from a nearby table and pulled it over next to Senna. She half-rose to greet him with a two-cheek kiss. Still standing, Senna introduced him to her friends. He had forgotten their names before he'd even finished the round of introductions. He sat down next to Senna.

"*Alors, ça va?*" she asked?

Felix felt a little uncomfortable answering back in English in so very French a setting, but he replied:

"Yes thanks, you?"

"Yes," she smiled.

"Were you working today?" he asked, trying to force

76

some form of flow into the conversation.

"Yes, from early," she replied, "you didn't come."

"Nah," said Felix, trying to make it sound uncalculated, "I went to Montparnasse,"

"Ah, very beautiful," she smiled. He was relieved when she pointed to a girl across the table.

"So this is my best friend, I know her since ten years," she said proudly, then leaned across to share a high five with the girl. Felix hadn't the courage to ask for her name again.

"And the others?"

She went round the table outlining how she knew everyone as Felix's knees melted as she spoke in her mild French accent. It was a good thing he was sitting down. She omitted one guy, sitting down the other end of the table. Felix didn't know what to make of that.

"So, tourist, 'ow long do you stay in Paris?" she turned to him, smiling cheekily as if knowing the term would rile him.

"Don't know. Maybe a few days, maybe longer." Felix admitted. He was sitting dry and decided it was time for a drink.

"What are you drinking?" he asked her.

"White wine,"

"Dry, I take it?"

"Yes, dry," she said, "why?"

But Felix was out of his chair by now and just smiled at her. The place was wide and cavernous, with a wooden bar stretching the length of the room, until it disappeared under the stairs that led to further seating upstairs. Bar staff were thin on the ground considering how many thirsty souls there were inside. As he stood with one elbow on the bar, he looked back at the table and saw Senna talking to her friend across the table, who looked his way and made eye contact, said something to Senna, then giggled and looked away. Felix smiled to himself, then ordered the drinks and headed back to the table. His bringing back a *pinte* struck a chord with the other guys at the table, who cannoned French banter his way until Senna told them, presumably, that he didn't speak French and they quickly died down. Felix noticed the others were drinking their beers out of chalices, glass goblets tall and slender, while his pint glass stood fat and bulky in comparison. One French guy managed to get some English words out:

"*Very beeg,*" he said. Felix felt a mixture of pride and acceptance from the group. As hè sat down, he subconsciously slid his chair in close to Senna's. She was talking to the girl to her left, so Felix picked up his glass and chinked with the guy who'd just spoken to him.

"*Tranquille?*" the guy asked.

"Yes mate," Felix said, at ease. "You live around here?"

"I live in Paris, yes," the guy said. Felix didn't remember his name and it would soon pass the stage where it was okay to ask.

"You work?"

"I am a *waiteur,*" he replied. Was anyone in this city not?

"Same place as Senna?"

"*Euh,* excuse me?" he asked.

"Do you work in the same café as Senna?" Felix asked, waving a hand in her general direction. At the sound of her name, Senna swivelled.

"Are you speaking about me?" she asked. Again that accent.

"Only good things," Felix quipped, raising his eyebrows and flashing her a cheeky smile. He turned back to the guy on his right. "Sorry," he admitted, "I've completely forgotten your name."

"Jean-Luc," he said. Of course it was. "And yours?"

"Felix,"

"Ah yes, Félix."

In French, it sounded more artist than housecat, more interesting than protected. He found, he realised, in this new name a new kind of identity, a confidence he'd had buried deep but never uncovered under Felix. Could a name have such an impact on character?

"*Euh*, so, no," Jean-Luc interrupted Félix's musings. "I work in a bar near here."

"No work tonight then?"

"No," Jean-Luc said with a broad smile. "Today, it's *repos*," he put his palms together and held them beside his cocked head, indicating sleep.

"*Parfois, c'est necessaire*," Félix said.

"*Ah, il parle Francais!*" Jean-Luc cheered, clearly relieved of his reprieve from speaking English to this stranger all night.

"*Un petit peu*," Félix admitted.

"So you 'ave to practice" Jean-Luc was adamant. "Hey, Senna," he started, then rattled off what had just happened. She looked at him playfully, challenging him to break his mould.

Félix looked back, unsure of what to do: insist on English, struggle on in French, or wait, frozen in the headlights until the scene blew over. After seconds that felt like years, Senna laughed, slapped him on the arm with the back of her hand and said "*C'est pas grave.*"

Félix wasn't sure what he was being let off from but he took the opportunity of Senna's attention to engage her. For lack of anything better to say but driven on by a desire to ride this out rather than let this fizzle out, he started, "Cool bar here," Corny? Lame?

"Yes, I like it," Senna replied. "I used to work here so we get free drinks."

In the end it really didn't matter what you said, so long as you said something.

"Always useful – next round's on you then," Félix grinned, then leaned back in his chair. Her English was thankfully better than Jean-Luc's, and he could play cocky comments off with a grin, without having to explain what he meant each time.

"Sure," Senna raised her eyebrows suggestively.

"So why did you quit?" Was it just him, or was their eye contact lingering?

"I didn't like working late – drunk people, too much noise, long hours," she said.

"You sound like you're fifty,"

"Hah, no – I was 'ere for a long time, but I prefer mornings," she said.

"So do I, I can just never get out of bed." Again that eye

80

contact lingered. Had he stirred his own interest with the mention of bed?

"It is easy work now, quiet – a few dumb *touristes* who come by for coffee," she nudged him with her arm. "So you want a drink?" she said, noticing his emptying glass.

"Wouldn't say no," Félix said, and got up to go to the bar with her – partly to decide what he'd have, partly to have her to himself. Senna greeted the barman and turned to Félix, who ordered a rum & coke. Senna made it two, then leaned into his ear and said over the sound of the bar: "Good choice."

Félix was enjoying the excitement of this chase: the will-it-won't-it, the yes and no swapping roles like a traffic light changing. She really was a most sophisticated being. Her white jacket flung over her shoulders hung slightly too high on one side, confessing the casual nature in which she'd pulled it on. Underneath was a neckline and shirt colour-co-ordinated to perfection to match her smooth bronzed skin. For the first time, he noticed several piercings in her ears.

"I like your earrings," he said.

"Thanks," she replied.

"Did you get addicted after one?"

"Sort of, yes," Senna said, "but it is in the family – we all have many, even my brother."

It hung more of a story, Félix thought, more intrigue, more exoticism around her shoulders. She touched them self-conciously, then ran her hand through her dark hair.

"*Santé*," she said, their eyes and glasses meeting again. She made no move to go back to the table.

"So what are you doing in Paris?" she asked.

"Oh, I'm just a dumb touriste," Félix quipped, "but I love the city."

"Really?" she said, "I'd love to leave."

"Why don't you?"

"My life is here, my work, my family…" she trailed off, as if leaving something unsaid. "And for you? Where is home?"

"London," Félix said.

"Wow," she said, clearly awed. "I love London!"

Félix guessed she'd only ever seen a tourist's view of London, and told her as much.

"Maybe – but it's amazing. You can be my tour guide next time."

"You have yourself a deal," he said, stretching out his hand to her. She took it in hers, soft and cared for, shook it and kept hold of it, again, a second longer than normal. When Félix dropped it, the feeling lingered, as if something was missing in the emptiness of his palm. The bar area was busy and thirsty punters pushed on his back, nudging him ever closer to Senna. With anyone else he'd have found this uncomfortable, but with this girl he'd met mere days before, it added to the thrill. He felt his heart quicken at the possibilities that shot off from this moment forward like sparks off a firework.

"You smoke?" he asked her.

"Normally no," Senna said.

"So that's a yes?" Félix barely waited for an answer, took his drink and headed towards the door of the bar. There was a deserted alleyway next to the bar. As Félix pulled out his cigarettes, he offered one to Senna. She considered for a moment, then took it. As Félix held out the lighter to her, she cupped her hands and again he felt her hands over his. His adrenaline stepped up a notch. This had to be, didn't it? Could he be misreading all these signs? Women were strange creatures and he'd been here often enough to know it could still go both ways. She blew smoke out, sideways, elegantly, then caught Felix looking at her.

"*Quoi*?"

"Nothing."

She took a step closer, into his face now.

"Tell me."

So Felix did – and before he knew it he felt the soft touch of skin on skin, lips on lips, and all that had gone before in the buildup to this, all that anxiety suddenly falling away around his closed eyes as he lived through his lips, directing the whole sum of his existence through them, stripping everything else of importance – this beautiful city, Alexander, all fell away into deep insignificance. He felt her hand on his waist, pulling him in and deeper, further still into the world of purest Senna, spreading through him like a drug –

– and then she tore away. Opening his eyes instinctively, he found himself back in the deserted alleyway, cigarette smouldering in his hand. He leaned in again, but Senna turned her head playfully, took a long drag of her cigarette and blew out over his shoulder. She looked at him, biting her lip. God, was she sexy. Playing the game exactly the way she knew would make him want her even more. To abstain from purest ecstasy on her lips now was to flounder in the gutter like the burning ember of a cigarette. With his free hand, he stroked gently down her ear, glancing a number of the earrings on the way. She arched her shoulders, smiling as would a cat being stroked. Reaching the lobe of her ear, he continued down her jawline, tracing it towards him, never breaking eye contact, until he reached her chin, lifted it towards his face, then leaned in and felt again that magical touch, slow at first, controlled, seductive, moving ever faster, handing over more and more control to emotion, tangling, spinning in a world far from here, feeling not the cold nor even his feet on the ground, feeling only those contact points with her, his hand slowly moving down to her side, reciprocating the tug, feeling the contours of her back through the thin material of her top, as their movements became more and more frenzied, less and less withheld until they danced, somewhere far up in the starry skies over Paris, or London, or any other city in the world. Felix paused, stroking her nose with his own, their eyes meeting again mere centimetres from each other, so close he couldn't even really focus.

"You're gorgeous," he whispered.

A small smile. "Do that again."

Taking a last drag of his cigarette, he tossed it to the edge of the alleyway, then reached up and touched the top of her right ear, free of piercings, lingering longer as she purred with the pleasure of it, tracing down her neck then tracing it back up to her lips where he rested his fingers briefly on her lips, still wet, and she kissed them gently. Then she took his hand, pulled him towards her, kissed him again for a brief moment, then turned on her heel and headed out of the alleyway back to the bar. Félix stood there, breathless. Senna looked back, put a single finger to her lips and was gone, back into the busy bar. Félix steadied himself on the wall, took a few deep breaths staring at the ground, and then followed Senna back in. Where would the night take him?

Back in the bar, the pair played it safe. Senna's leg sat against his, while drink after drink went in, and Felix ended up talking to most of the group in turn. Everyone, it seemed, but Senna. She was conspicuous in her coldness, but their sharing of a secret kept the balloon of excitement inflated. It was clear Senna didn't want her friends to know what had transpired outside – that was to remain a secret kept between him, her and the night. When they did speak, it was as if nothing had happened.

Several hours later, there were just the four of them left – him, Senna, Jean-Luc, for whom alcohol had transcended any language barrier, and another, quite pretty, friend of Senna's called Louisa. Félix guessed by looking at her she was Portuguese. Eventually, she too got up to go. Jean-Luc lingered as last rounds were called. Félix was now in for the ride and suggested the three of them do one more – "for the road" was an expression he had to explain to them. She said no, it was 2am and she'd seen enough. Outside, Félix shook Jean-Luc's hand by way of a formal farewell. With Senna, he stood watching Jean-Luc, as his silhouette cut a solitary path down the street. In the three hours since that kiss, Félix's expectations had dimmed, perhaps as an act of self-pres-ervation, defence against any disappointment later in the night. Now though, he found himself once more daring to hope for more. As soon as Jean-Luc turned a corner, Senna was in his face, her hands grasping at his neck, the collar of his shirt, pulling him back into her world, this time free from the control and romanticism that had laced their first kiss. Pulling away briefly, Félix breathed the words, "I want you," into her ear, teasing her earlobe with his teeth.

"Come," Senna took his hand and led him away in the opposite direction to where Jean-Luc had gone. Félix had no better plan than to follow. A vast freedom lay open to him, to go and do what he pleased, with nothing in the world to be late for, and no one to answer to but his conscience, by now quite inebriated. He shuddered at the thrill of it, the unspoken chase still very much on, leading him God knew where into the night. Their ten-minute walk was punctuated by pauses, up against walls, parked cars and in bus shelters, until Senna stopped outside a tall apartment block and typed a number into the keypad beside the door. A click resonated from inside and Senna let them into a dark entry hall and up four flights of carpeted stairs that wound around in a loose spiral. Félix felt more and more anticipation as he strayed further and further into unknown territory. A second door led down a pitch black corridor and finally into a dimly-lit studio; a kitchen, living room and dining room in one. Without thinking to remove his coat, he pushed Senna down onto the bed and dived at her neck with his lips.

They lay, tangled, sweaty, out of breath, Félix's hand stroking Senna's back as her head rose and fell on his chest.

She looked up at him, her brown eyes burning into his.

"I should probably tell you something," her voice breaking the silence that had fallen over them like a duvet. Félix drew his head back, trying to anticipate what was to come. Senna remained quiet for a moment. The silence had turned from a duvet into a giant balloon, inflating all the while between their two naked bodies.

"I have a boyfriend," she said finally.

Felix took his hand off her back and pushed her away in reflex. "*What?*"

"Yes," Senna confirmed.

"But –" Felix said, then fell silent. So much was thrown into question with that one statement that he didn't know where to start.

"I know," Senna said. She didn't sound the least bit ashamed. Then, judging the impending questions, "but this is different."

"But what if he finds out?" Felix picked to be his first question.

"Then he finds out. That's okay."

"I don't understand," Felix said.

Senna was now back at his side, stroking his face, her voice soothing.

"Don't worry," she chuckled reassuringly, "I loved it."

"Then why are you with him?" Felix asked.

"Like I said, it's different. Tonight was amazing and so exciting." She put one leg over him and sat on his stomach, with no effort to cover up. "But what I have with him is special – a long-term thing, someone safe."

"Okay…" Felix still wasn't understanding.

"But it's not per se exciting – not like this," she leaned down, her breasts stroking Felix's chest as her lips brushed his. Felix, irked, twisted his head away.

"But isn't that how relationships tend to go?" Felix asked, rhetorically.

"Yeah, but why give up on the excitement? Why have either-or when you can have both?"

"Cause it just…doesn't work like that," Felix said after a moment's thought.

"As sure as I'm sitting here it does." She traced a line down from his lips, past his chin to where she sat on his stomach. Despite his confusion, Felix was still aroused.

"See, it's exciting," she grinned. "Why give that up?"

"Most people aren't keen on their partners sleeping around," Felix said.

"That, Felix, is a matter of communication." She had the tone of a teacher. She climbed off him, lay down and in the dark found his lips with hers. Within minutes he was inside her again.

*

As she slept, he got up, filled a glass of water and stood by the window, feeling the breeze cool on his body. He believed her, yes – how could he not after what had happened – but did he *understand*? Below the window, air-conditioning units grumbled in the night, a backdrop to his disquiet mind. A string of words entered his head unasked for and stayed there, looping like a sample, tormenting him like a mosquito in his ear. "*What a night, and yet, what absolutely not a night.*" The words swum in his head, taking on new meaning with every repetition. He found a form of poetic solace in the form of the words, watching them visibly written out on his brain as if in his own handwriting in a notebook, the n's flowing into the d's, the t's crossed all slapdash. He looked around, back in the room. In the glow that crept up from the street, he saw clothes strewn over the floor. He passed his eyes over his jeans, her bra and then her, succumbed to sleep at last, defeated on the bed.

"What a night, and yet, what absolutely not a night," he repeated to himself as he lay later, inhaling Senna's scent in her neck. It was a select few, he mused, who got this close to another human being, close enough to smell the perfume on her skin. Maybe it was different with this girl. Still the line tormented him. He felt troubled by a certain unfinished business, a certain unease that the words would come so easily in the morning, if at all. His mind growled as his stomach would if hungry. His thoughts less and less coherent, he drifted in a world between worlds, caught up in waves of sleep, still feeling Senna's peaceful rising and falling beside him. The line would need to wait.

He slept lightly, waking every time Senna turned over. By the time the sun rose, Felix was more tired than when he'd gone to bed. He got up again to cover the windows, and leaned out, still naked, to close the shutters. The calming of the infernal machines below meant he could hear a distant church chime seven. As he stood in the darkened room, he thought how no one would fully know the rollercoaster that had been last night but he and Senna. Torn, he stood momentarily caught between liberation and loneliness.

Sometime during the night, Senna had pulled her underwear back on, and they sat stark black, complementing the curve of her hips. He'd left at this stage before, tiptoeing out, his hair still a mess, his teeth unbrushed. On one occasion he'd realised half-way down the street, with a sinking stomach, that his wallet still lay on the girl's bedside table. He considered leaving it. It was only when he realised he'd also left his keys and couldn't get into his house that he returned with his tail between his legs. She'd handed them back to him at the door in her dressing-gown, a smug smile on her face.

Yet he couldn't bring himself to leave. He was intrigued by Senna and the way she thought. Was this a mindset he should be adopting? Was this a life that his mind, such as it was, could even handle adopting? Questions buzzed on his brain, which still felt foggy from the night before. But while he was here, he decided, he might as well treat her right – there was no point fretting about the situation if she clearly didn't. After all, it was she who had lured him in, it was her story to tell, her conscience to face up to. He reminded himself that he'd be out of the city in a few days, but when confronted by that thought, realised he didn't want to leave.

Senna still lay asleep, the duvet covering her leg, her breasts exposed. He found her keys lying on the metal worktop of the kitchen. He got dressed and slipped out of the house. Outside was as he liked it, early doors – *fresh air and empty streets.* Another sentence had written itself into his mind. It was shaping up to be a rare glorious day, and the air felt liberating, like stepping out of a cave of sin into a fresh scene of purity. As he walked along the pedestrian avenue, Felix felt he was floating on air – not air perhaps but something like it, something heavier that blurred the lines between thought and reality, something that blurred even the boundaries between reality and reality itself, warping what he thought to be solid into watery shapes – yes, more like water than air – shifting his perspective from solid atoms forming shape and truth into a hesitant in-between mess, putting question marks at the end of sentences where there had previously been full-stops, adding semi-colons of continuity instead of dots of finality.

He turned left, heading down a mosaic-paved street. He kept his sight on the horizon, peering out for a sign of life in one of the shops on the road ahead. After about five minutes of walking, he came upon a 24-hour shop. Behind the till, the owner was listening to a grainy radio. Felix meandered around the shop and picked up breakfast and then, remembering Senna, doubled up the croissants in his basket and stooped to pick up a punnet of strawberries.

The owner of the shop barely acknowledged Felix as he scanned and weighed the goods, grunting a price at Felix. Felix handed over five euros – the only noteworthy money that had survived last night's onslaught. He received minimal change. Outside Senna's apartment block he found a bench and sat down. What a different girl he knew in Senna now to the girl he'd met cleaning tables at the *Café au Jardins.*

He could scarcely put the two together, barely accommodate both of them in the body of that one girl. By the time he let himself back in, Senna had turned and covered herself. She'd left no indication she'd missed him, but he couldn't bring himself to lie down next to her again. He was awake now, more or less, and didn't want to waste the day in bed, despite the effects of the night before echoing on his body and brain. He pulled a plate from the drying-up rack, put the croissants on it and took the strawberries over in their punnet, placing them down on their brown paper bag on her sheets. He put a hand on her shoulder and shook her. Her eyes opened, then opened wider as she saw what he'd got for her.

"Mmmm," a mutter of surprise escaped her lips, heavy from sleep. She sat up, pulled the sheets around herself and kissed him by way of a thank you. Tucking into breakfast, she smiled at him. After a few moments of satisfied silence, she trusted her vocal cords to form words.

"Thank you." She sounded genuinely grateful.

Felix eventually left the house around midday. Outside, in real-life Paris, tourists were already halfway through their day, had seen half the city at whistle-stop speed, stopping only to tick whatever monument stood in front of them off some list in their mind before hurrying away to the next one, lest daylight failed before they'd seen everything their guidebook told them to. By removing the burden of expectation that tourists hung around Paris' neck – by it never even existing in the first place – he'd found a place more real, more alive, far less rigid than the guidebook city. For that at least, he was grateful.

The shops he'd seen setting up when he first went out were now bustling. That delightful morning hour was long gone and lunch service was in full swing. Put off by the crowds, Felix kept walking until he reached the river again, watching its power flowing as it did, caught between the city's banks. He crossed the river at the Pont des Arts, heaving under the weight of the love and responsibility it carried, its fate pulling the bridge riverwards while city planners brandished wirecutters at every opportunity. Vendors of the cheapest kind of lock stood on the bridge eagerly, but not one even made eye contact with Felix. He ambled, hands in coat pockets, spinning a fifty cent piece between his fingers. His heels beat down on the wooden boards of the bridge, drumming the rhythm of his nonchalant progress. Reaching the Rive Gauche, he found a bench and sat watching the river and the passers-by.

For the next half-hour, Felix's thoughts flitted around Senna's outlook. Could he possibly adopt a stance of loving detachment? With regret, he doubted it.

*

The pair met at the entrance of the *Tuileries* and wandered through towards the museum. Alexander had been late, and Felix had by now stopped being surprised. A gust of wind blew clouds of sand across the open space, palm trees quivered like birds' tail feathers, their rustling sounding like light rain. On the museum's forecourt, the pyramid caught the clouds as they passed by on the glass, white against an otherwise bright blue panel. The fountains clattered in the background. A small girl in a white sunhat ran over and threw a coin into the water.

Alexander signalled to Felix to sit. Felix moved to the edge of the fountain and sat down. Alexander sat beside him and pulled a bottle out of his bag. It must have been one of the most highly-patrolled areas of the city. Felix glanced over his shoulder. Alexander shrugged.

"We'll do the Louvre the artists' way."

Felix twisted the bottle, pulled out the cork and raised it to his lips tentatively. He felt it warm and sweet on the way down. Port. He coughed and wiped his lips with the back of his hand.

Alexander handed over two cards to the museum staff, who gave them half a glance and let them both pass without payment.

Felix had to focus on keeping his balance on the steps as he walked up. He stumbled once, putting his hand down onto the cold stone to steady himself. By the time he reached the top he was out of breath. In the first room the pair came to, Felix stood amazed. Carved out of marble were lifelike creations as if time itself had frozen them where they stood. Robes flowed around ankles, bunches of flowers lay freshly-picked in a mourning woman's hand, lifelike fingers curled around a paper scroll, waves rolled under a storming galleon.

Amidst this storm of stationary beauty, a girl stood, back to the world, absorbed in sketching a statue of a wounded soldier. Felix couldn't see her face, but instantly knew her to be beautiful. A glance at her paper indicated she was quite accurate with the pencil too. Felix and Alexander moved on, Alexander raising his eyebrows, Felix nodding in confirmation.

As they wandered the halls of the majestic palace, side-stepping small children, Felix was startled at the place's grandeur. Every pillar was decorated, every ceiling painted, every bit of stonework embellished. A droning hum hung in the air of thousands of bodies admiring work of an ancient hand, punctuated occasionally by shoes squeaking on the polished marble or a camera shutter clicking shut. The sound reminded Felix of the echoing sound of life sometimes heard inside a cathedral. Indeed, it was in many ways a cathedral to masters gone before, to the intricacies of human expression, to the hours put in to create beauty out of the Earth. Signs on the wall directed visitors to various eras or styles, or in one case, a small world-famous painting of a lady whose eyes supposedly followed you across the room. Stumbling upon it quite by accident, the pair were confronted by hordes, as if the whole population of the museum had come to see this miniature painting, far smaller than Felix had ever imagined. How this small canvas had captured the collective imagination of the world was beyond him, and by Alexander's scathing glance, it was clear he didn't think much of it either. The crowd was so deep that most at the back were craning their neck or holding up cameras with the lens extended in order to catch a glimpse.

"That's what you get when you let experts decide the value of art – when fund managers select art based on resale value rather than artistic merit." Alexander said. It sounded part jealous, part bitter at what the top of the art world had become. "It's not even really art anymore. It's an investment." He spat the word out as if it left a horrible taste in his mouth. "Money destroys every trace of beauty."

Felix couldn't help but agree. In the short time they'd been in the museum he'd already seen far superior pieces, both ancient and alive. Through an upstairs window, Felix saw the earlier clouds on the pyramid replaced by glittering sunlight, dancing up off the fountains shimmering in the warming air.

"Let's push on," he said. Alexander nodded. They pressed on through more halls, stopping every now and then to admire a particularly striking canvas. They wandered for about ten minutes through long corridors with no end, past masterpieces with no end to their skill. The museum went on forever. Eventually, Alexander made an exclamation.

The room that had provoked Alexander's relief went off at right-angles to the endless hall they had been in. It was long and rectangular with an elongated skylight above a long low leather bench down the middle. Along the walls hung giant canvases like shirts off the backs of giants.

"Rubens," Alexander said proudly, as if he had had a hand in their creation.

Felix looked around, unsure of where to start taking in. Stepping over to a painting, he examined the minute details on every square inch of this enormous cloth. Each depiction was crammed to the edges with the most intricate details, and that which made up the heart of the image was of equally fine quality. Each must have taken weeks to produce. Felix moved down the hall, pausing to take in each one anew, finding the same obsessive level of details and quality right to the frame of each one. The room was a temple to the man painted by his own hand. By the time Felix reached the end of the row, he was in absolute awe of this artist who had devoted so much time to producing beauty in its purest form. It must have taken years of practice and days of concentration, not to mention considerable natural talent. Felix found himself wishing there was something in his life that was comparable, that he'd give everything up for, to spend hours doing that and just that. But there simply wasn't. He was ruled by inactivity and layers of apathy. And it was here, as he stood with that thought in mind, that a revelation hit him, as if a beam of light had come through the skylight and shone straight into the dusty corners of his assumptions. A man who gave up everything in pursuit of a passion – that was Alexander's story, pure and simple. This longing – once thought and which could never be unthought – was exactly what Alexander had gone through. Realisation hit him like a tonne of bricks, shattering his skylight of moral high-ground as suddenly, *suddenly* he was reduced to Alexander's level, yet simultaneously elevated by the very thought of it. The love of something so strong as to guide your every move, as to dictate your every action and thought – this was not something to be frowned upon, rather something empowering, something to be embraced. Yet at the same time, the thought unnerved him. Had he implicitly condoned Alexander's behaviour? Did this desire for a passion, this realisation of Alexander's motives mean that Felix accepted his behaviour, perhaps even stood behind it? Suddenly torn between his mother's world and Alexander's, he stood, staring straight ahead without even realising he was in a gallery, a miles-away look on his face, seeing, feeling, experiencing Alexander's side for the first time. He felt his knees weak – weaker than they already were from the afternoon's drinking – and moved to sit down, psychological-ly winded as if hit in the chest with a giant hammer.

Alexander could tell something was up and dragged himself away from one of Rubens' masterpieces to come over.

"Are you alright?" he asked.

"I don't know." It came out as more of an exhalation than a statement, as Felix gasped for air and understanding. Alexander sat down next to Felix in silence.

"I – understand," Felix uttered at last. "It's all clear, and I wish it weren't."

Still Alexander said nothing. He realised Felix was on something heavy, a realisation that had temporarily taken the life out of him. Felix struggled still – like a plastic bag caught on a high wire his conscience flapped on thoughts he could no longer unthink. It was no good, the thought had crossed his mind, the understanding had set in and he was in for the ride, wherever it may take him.

Finally he said: "I know – I know why you left Mum."

"You do?" Alexander asked.

"Yes –" Felix said. Suddenly blinking, suddenly sure, he turned to look at his father. "When I saw Rubens, I wished I had that kind of drive, that kind of passion that would push me to such lengths as to create greatness and be hung in a museum, to leave some remnant of myself walking the Earth after I was long gone – to squeeze every drop of talent out of this body I've been given, to devote myself entirely to a cause I felt so strongly about that I'd give up anything – everything – to pursue it."

If Felix had looked up, he'd have seen Alexander trying to contain a smile.

"And then – and then," Felix paused. He had trouble getting the words out, as if by saying them he would cement them in reality forever. "And then I thought of what you said in the bar the first night we met – about your 'beast' – and I realised I'd just wished the same beast upon myself."

"You understand," more a statement than a question.

"I have no choice but to," Felix said, "I've lured myself into a trap of thoughts, a trap of logic so compelling, that I now can't not understand. I can't put all these twos and twos together and *not* understand."

"Mmm," said Alexander, seemingly agreeing with Felix, but it was clear something was still bothering the young man.

"But something's troubling you about it."

"Yes," said Felix, "For so long I've lived with Mum, hearing how you jilted us, left us to choke while you swanned off following your dreams – what about *our* dreams of a happy family?" Felix was already swaying back towards his mother's side. What was right and what was wrong was being batted back and forth in his mind so fast that even the most experienced umpire couldn't possibly keep up.

"I always saw her in the right, that she was the one wronged, that we were the ones left behind. And she was, there's no denying that, we both were, but –" Felix babbled, then stumbled again, sighing with the resigned realisation of what he was about to say, "but, you were right too."

A long silence followed. Felix dropped his head into his hands and stared at his shoes on the polished wood floor. They hardly felt like his feet anymore, save the remnants of his night at the Sacré-Cœur which still flecked them. What right did Vivienne have to keep Alexander there against his will? Besides the moral obligation to ensure his son had a good upbringing – and had Felix not had that with Vivienne? – Alexander had acted out of egocentrism, certainly, but what would his life have been like if he hadn't?

"It's just hard to realise that what you see as the truth for so long can be undone by your own mind in such a big way," Felix finally offered up. "I still don't really want to understand it – it was much easier having a side chosen for me from birth." Silence. "Now I don't know what's right and what's wrong." He felt he was at the centre of rushing rapids, cascading over rocks, being pulled every which way, most of all downwards. His moral compass had been hit by a magnet of understanding, and his head spun with the consequences.

All around the pair, tourists passed by without a care in the world, unaware, blissfully unaware of the landslide that had just occurred in Felix's mind that left him with nowhere to go – swaying on a tightrope of truth and subjectivity. Was there then, he wondered, an absolute truth in this situation? Was there then an absolute truth *anywhere* in the universe? He looked back at Rubens, this dead master who had brought all this on. He saw a new angle to the work now, a lifetime of choices, picking art above everything else, a never-ending quest for ever-greater perfection. It had cost Alexander his family. What had it cost Rubens? What had it cost the cumulative artist, stretching back to the first person to put pen to paper or brush to canvas? The losses must be equal to that of war – and indeed it was a sort of war; an internal struggle between two passions. Did the neglected love ever really go away, as art had refused to go away for Alexander, if ignored?

"Do you ever wonder what your life would look like if you'd stayed?" Felix's thoughts had sped on since he'd last spoken, and his seeming change of subject took Alexander by surprise.

"Yes," Alexander said after a moment's thought, "Yes I do."

"How do you picture it?"

"Happy – in parts," Alexander said. "I had a loving wife who obviously cared very deeply for you, as did – do – I," Alexander corrected himself. "I was just afraid her undying love for me was waning. I was afraid she couldn't have enough love in her for two men in her life, that her love was a scarce resource. If I'd stayed? Who knows. Quite likely things would have gone back to how they were, with you melding seamlessly into the family, but perhaps I'd have become more and more of an outsider – caught between art and Vivienne, yet not attaining either. We'll never know now, will we?" he said with a half-ironic laugh.

Felix shrugged.

"I don't know if my desire to paint would ever really go away, so ingrained in me has it now become. Looking back, I couldn't imagine *not* painting. It's just so many things to me," he said, answering the question Felix had not asked.

"Do you still love Vivienne?" Felix was surprised at the boldness of his question to a man he was only just coming to know.

From Alexander's face, it looked like it was a question he'd been expecting, but when it came he didn't know what to do with it. "It's something I've tried not to think about. The more thought I gave it, the more I questioned my decision. Then I'd turn back to my easel, pick up a paintbrush, and I would know I had made the right choice. But given the chance to fall in love again, I may well. Not that that's ever going to happen." He paused and turned to Felix. "Look Felix, both were strong to the point of being all-encompassing, and the energy, time and passion I was putting into each when they were the only thing, was entire, complete. There simply wasn't space for another."

Felix looked puzzled. "I don't really understand," he said.

"No Felix," Alexander admitted, "nor, really, do I. To tell you the truth, I made my decision based on a feeling. When Vivienne wanted a rational explanation I couldn't give her one. It was a feeling. I felt like a failure for my inability to give her a reason she could understand. But how do you properly put words to a feeling like that?"

You do it the way you did to me, Felix thought. Let me live it, let me realise it and I'll understand.

"I felt like a failure," Alexander repeated. "I felt that one of the biggest ways I let her down was in not getting her to understand." He dropped his head with a sigh of remembrance. "But then, is there ever full understanding of a break-up? Relationships exist on emotion, and all of a sudden you're expected to explain things in a way that makes rational sense. Oftentimes you can't."

Felix was beginning to have a lot more time for Alexander's sorrow and was coming to realise his sadness was a byproduct of his struggle to do the right thing for irreconcilable parties. Something had had to give. He and Vivienne had been the collateral damage on the battlefield of thoughts that had raged in Alexander's head, a battle that still raged if he let it.

"Do you think you'll ever truly make peace with the decision?" Felix asked.

Alexander shrugged, a terribly involved shrug. "I don't know, Felix," he said with a wince, as if the admission hurt him. "I always thought it would come through painting. I always think achieving something great is a very powerful step in overcoming sadness. But I've achieved. My paintings sell, I can live off them and I'm living in Paris as a bloody artist. What more achievement could I desire? I've no ambitions to be famous, that much I've made clear to you. But despite this success, despite this confirmation of my talent, trying to run from what I've done through success just *hasn't* worked. And how did I ever really believe that it would? Out there, there's still a woman whose heart I've broken, still a child who never had a father. And it's my fault."

It was poignant that the breakthrough had come in an art museum, as if Felix could only really understand when confronted by the very thing he had lost Alexander to. They sat for a few more moments in silence, until Felix said abruptly,

"Let's go."

His revelation had rendered the museum unremarkable, and with other things on his mind he didn't want to wander the halls any longer. They made their way out. Felix walked with a feeling of distance, as if his body was no longer his. Broken loose from his unerring belief that Vivienne was completely right and Alexander completely wrong, situations to him now became a game of perspectives and misunderstanding. He felt directionless, as if the one key truth in his life had suddenly exploded in a puff of reason, and he now didn't know whether to laugh or cry. He wanted to be alone. To do anything now, anything at all, would feel trivial. To slip back into ordinary life would be as if it had all been for nothing, as if his realisation and the blow it had dealt him were somehow not real and he could go about his normal life without them getting in the way. On the other hand, sitting stewing would not help anything either. His world had fallen from concrete certainties into a plague of question marks buzzing around his head. His future opened up like a gigantic black hole, a long tunnel of baseline existence. He didn't know. He didn't know anything. His mind spun in a storm of lifelong uncertainty.

What he needed was a trusted friend, someone to get his thoughts off his conscience and clear in his brain. Besides Roger, he knew no one in this city. And Roger was more a friend to Alexander than he was to Felix. Dangerous territory. Senna?

"I'm off – somewhere," Felix said as they stepped outside. The last few days seemed like a blur of hard-to-process lessons and confrontational meetings. "I'll call you," he said, leaving Alexander in the lurch. Tough, thought Felix. He'd decided to choose for himself.

*

An hour later, he found himself sitting in a café back in Montmartre. He'd dropped into a *tabac* for pen and paper. He opened the notebook up on the table in front of him. Briefly he froze – how was he supposed to do this? The blank page stared up at him, unblinking. He'd only ever written when told to, and even then only on a set topic, but he felt he had words to say that needed saying to someone, *something*, so he picked up his pen and started writing. His thoughts were jumbled, jarring with his morals, the see-saw of reason continually tipping every which way in his mind. He wrote freely, letting whatever words were in his brain tumble onto the paper in whatever order they came out. He wrote of his struggle between right and wrong, his questioning of the whole concept of absolute truths and the implications for his continuing life. After scribbling several pages, he sat back, out of breath, hand aching. He shook it to loosen it up and caught the waiter's eye for another beer. Sitting back, he read back over what he'd written. The ideas were there, but in a jumbled mess, with sentences stretching half the page, bits crossed out, words all out of order. This was a terrible representation of the revelation he'd had, he thought to himself, almost disgusted at what he'd put down on paper. He flipped the notebook shut. How pretentious he'd been, spouting this rubbish into the expensively-bought notebook. He sat looking out of the window at the materials shop opposite, long rolls of garish uncut material hung on the doors and along the walls. The waiter brought the beer he hardly remembered ordering and Felix sat staring, hardly even thinking, occasionally raising the glass to his lips, almost automatically. When he'd finished, he paid, took his notebook and headed back to the hotel. He felt so annoyed he could spit, tear the notebook up as he wished he could go back to before he'd bought it, before he'd found an art form he was so rubbish at. He cursed his inability to write, for who would ever want to read this?!

It was 7pm. If he hadn't got out of bed this morning, Felix thought, none of this would have happened. He'd still be comfortably annoyed at Alexander, he wouldn't have disturbed a hive of question marks buzzing around his brain and he wouldn't have kicked his self-esteem to smithereens in his attempt at writing. He reached for his phone.

*

"Are you around?"

"Yes,"

"Can I come over?"

"Sure,"

Half an hour later he arrived at her building. He buzzed the door, heard it click and pushed it inwards. He was halfway up the second set of stairs by the time his eyes adjusted to the gloom of the interior. She was waiting for him on the landing of the fourth set and greeted him with a kiss. Felix broke away, breathing hard from the climb.

"You okay?" she asked.

"I don't know," Felix replied.

"Come in," Senna said.

She led him into her studio and sat down, her right leg folded under her left, which swung casually from the bed.

"*Dis-moi.*"

He knew that when he started, it would all need to come out. He took a breath and told her. He told her of growing up in a single-parent family, of how it had affected his mother, of how he'd despised Alexander for what he'd done, of his anger turning to curiosity as he grew older, of the arguments he'd had with his mother as he planned to visit Paris, of how it had almost put him off coming, of his finally meeting Alexander and eventually of his revelation mere hours before at the Louvre.

Throughout the story, Senna had sat attentively watching him. As he ended, he moved to apologise.

"And I hardly know you and here I am burdening you with my problems already. I'm sorry," he blurted. He felt mentally weak at what he'd just done.

Senna just smiled then stood up, opening her arms to him.

"Don't apologise."

He stood and they embraced silently, Felix's ear against Senna's, the smell of her hair his entire world. As seconds ticked into minutes, Felix stepped away, keeping his hands on Senna's waist.

"Thank you," he smiled at her.

"So what now?" Senna asked.

Felix turned towards the open window. "I don't know."

"How is your mum doing?"

Felix hadn't spoken to her since he'd got to Paris.

"Same as ever, I suppose."

"It can't have been easy for her either."

"No, like I said, she was in pieces."

"I mean before then. Can you imagine the pressure? I can't imagine someone giving up their passion to be with me. It's a massive role to fill."

"I'd never even seen it like that."

The ball of reason swerved as it flew over the net again.

Later that night, as Senna lay her head on his chest, tracing her index finger over his skin, watching its path, she asked: "So how long are you staying?"

He thought about it. "When I first came I figured I'd stay as long as I needed. Now I'm not sure what it was that I needed in the first place." Was there something deeper in her question? "I'm not sure what staying longer will achieve. Life continues on back home."

"You have a father here," Senna said.

Felix was silent. Senna filled the blanket of silence.

"And me."

Ah, there *had* been.

She changed the subject. "How will your mum be to see you back?"

"Glad, I guess. At least I'll be back with her. But I fear there'll be something between us we may never clear up."

"But you have to make your own decisions – she has to understand that."

"I think she fears losing me like she did Alexander."

"I think you're mature enough to juggle two parents in your life."

Felix grinned, relieved, as if she'd cast light on the most obvious thing in the world.

"We'd better say a proper goodbye then, just in case," Senna looked up at him playfully.

*

She woke early for work the next morning, showered, dressed and stood in front of the bathroom mirror doing her make-up. Felix came in behind her and linked his hands around her stomach. She leaned back into him, turned and met his lips with hers.

As they left the apartment, the emptiness of the street embraced them. As they neared the *Café au Jardins* and conversation fell to silence, Senna turned to Felix.

"Bye," she said, putting her arms around his neck and

raising herself up on her toes to his height.

"Take care," Felix said. "And thanks."

Five minutes later, Senna left to start work. Felix went back to the hotel, opened his window to the slowly waking city, closed the curtains and lay down, hands folded beneath his head. By focussing on his chest rising and falling as he breathed, he found he could avoid the drifting thoughts of art, of Senna, of truth, of Alexander, of love, of Vivienne. He preferred it that way. Even if he tried, he wouldn't have known where to start drawing lines, or where to put full-stops.

A few hours later, Felix came to as his phone buzzed on the bedside table. Alexander.

"Hello?" Felix said.

"Hi Felix, it's Alexander," he heard down the line. "Fancy some lunch?"

"Why not?" Felix said. It would be a while before Alexander would get anywhere, and even then he'd probably be late. Felix wouldn't need to leave for a while yet.

"Go to *Bastille*. I'll meet you there at 2."

"Okay," said Felix, "If I'm there at 2:30 I won't have to wait."

Alexander laughed in recognition of a flaw he clearly didn't take too seriously. "I'll be there at 2."

Alexander reached in to hug Felix. Felix made no move to return the hug so Alexander ended up draping himself limply around Felix's shoulders, then retracted swiftly. They went down a backstreet which opened up onto a square of cobblestones with a quiet road running along one side of it.

Alexander gestured to a table at one of the nearby restaurants, shaking the hand of the waiter as pulled out a chair. After a quick chat, the waiter handed over two menus. Alexander didn't even open his. Felix looked down at it briefly, caught sight of a steak that would do him nicely and snapped the menu shut.

"Too early for a beer?" Alexander asked.

"Is it ever?" said Felix.

When the waiter came back they ordered.

"You know everyone here," Felix said.

Alexander tried to act modest, but smiled. "Not quite everyone, just those at my regular places," he replied.

"That's a lot of regular haunts," Felix said.

"What can I say?" Alexander said, "I'm out and about a lot. It's where I get my inspiration."

As he said that, Felix realised he had never seen one of Alexander's canvases. Until recently, it was the last thing he wanted to do, but he was now suddenly struck with a pang of curiosity.

"What do you actually paint?" Felix asked.

Alexander pursed his lips as if his face was shrugging at the question.

"All sorts of things, really," he finally replied, then thought again. "Yeah, a bit of everything. Anything from scenes of life, this kind of place –" he threw his thumb over his shoulder indicating the square they sat on, "– but also individuals. Some of my favourite pieces are those I've done of my artistic idols. I have them in my studio as a constant reminder of their genius. I suppose I hope they'll impart some of their talent on me." He laughed. "I've done some portraits on commission, but I never really enjoyed that too much. Sometimes I'll spot a shape and tell a story through its form, through its reflections, through its colours."

"Any particular style?"

"Would it mean anything to you if I told you?"

"No," Felix admitted, "it probably wouldn't."

"I'm not really one for putting art into particular boxes. My eye knows what I like when I see it." A motorbike's growl temporarily punctured the relative calm of the square. "How about I show you some after lunch? We can go to my place. That's probably where the biggest collection of my stuff will be."

"Sure," said Felix, as curious to see the inside of the man's house and how he lived as to see the paintings.

"I live about fifteen minutes from here,"

"I know," Felix said, "Roger took me there."

Alexander was taken aback. "What, when?"

"About a week ago, when I was first in the city," Felix said. "You didn't open up."

Alexander looked caught by a guilty secret and remained silent.

"So we went away again."

Alexander sat accused, the burden of silence building up on him.

"I didn't know what to do, Felix. I was...."

"And that's why you didn't show up to meet Roger and me, as well, eh?" He doubled up the helping of shame he

112

was dishing out.

Alexander couldn't make eye contact at first.

"Look Felix," he said, finally looking up. "To be frank, I was...I was scared. It was something from the past that I thought I'd put behind me."

"Afraid I'd drag up memories and disrupt your pleasant artistic existence? Was that it?" Felix demanded angrily.

Alexander said nothing, confirming Felix's thoughts with his silence. "Felix, I'm sorry. I just –" he trailed off, "I just didn't know it would be like this." Alexander spread his hands wide.

"Alexander, all I wanted was some answers. I've only been waiting fifteen years for them."

"I know. To have to have left you like that, for that long, is unforgiveable," Alexander seemed to visibly shrink as he sat there, shying away from the truth as if blinking back bright sunlight. Felix wondered whether he'd gone too far, but this was a truth that needed to be spoken.

Alexander picked himself up. "But I couldn't have hoped for anything as good as this. The way you've handled it has been nothing short of admirable. Yes, it hasn't been easy, but you've been frank and honest and maintained the morals your mother clearly brought you up with. Admirable – *really*."

Felix didn't feel too admirable, but saw that Alexander had made a valid point. It just wasn't in his nature to do any differently. He'd not had to decide to be honest, it was just who he was, doing what he needed to do. "Thank you." It lay somewhere on the line between sarcastic and genuine

113

gratitude, an observant kind of statement. "But don't think all is rosy and all is forgiven after three days."

"I wouldn't expect to be forgiven, not even after a lifetime. Sometimes though, I think that things are better left remembered, unforgiven. This decision was so entirely true to myself that to forgive and forget would rob me of a part of my identity."

Felix took this in, ponderously. It was a strange thing to want something that major to remain between them.

"It's a reminder every day of the consequences of one's actions, especially now the loop's closed and I've met you again. A reminder that sometimes, the right thing to do is the hardest thing to do."

"Mmm."

Alexander continued. "But then again – you have to question, right for who? Eventually it comes down to you. 'Cause if you don't look after yourself Felix, there's not a damn person who will." He seemed to be justifying it to himself again, the balance in his mind sliding back towards it being the right decision. At that point their beers arrived. They each sipped without chinking glasses.

After lunch, Alexander led the way to his house, passing a supermarket for a bottle of rum on the way. As Alexander unlocked the door, Felix could smell sharp chemicals in the air that drifted down the stairs. Alexander made no mention of it. Felix followed him up the curved staircase for several flights until they arrived at the second floor, into a room with two large windows at one end. One was propped open with a jam jar. A big table took up the middle of the room, scattered with tubes of paint, brushes, paper plates, sketchbooks, an overflowing ashtray and jars full of colourless liquid. The whole room, in fact, was a tip, a work in progress caught at its absolute messiest. Against the wall stood innumerable canvases, at least three rows deep, most unframed, some painted directly onto wooden panels. Some stood on thin shelves that ran along the walls, as an exhibition to the man in his own house.

"I ran out of space a little bit," Alexander spoke the obvious. Felix looked over the walls – his eyes resting on a street scene. He walked over to it, examining it closer, his eye drawn down the street to the figure walking into the sun, as buildings flanked the scene. It told a story in paint of a new beginning, of an unknown destination, of leaving the darkness behind and entering the light. At the same time, Felix saw it from the perspective of the one left behind, watching a loved one's silhouette disappear into the distance. The use of colour meant you didn't know, *couldn't* know, if it was daybreak or sunset. One thing was clear though: "Fresh air and empty streets," Felix said out loud.

"What?"

Felix repeated it. "That's what I'd call this painting."

"I like it – very poetic." Alexander said. "Do you like it?"

"Yes, I do. The universality of this scene and the story it tells. It's a whole life in one painting."

"It was an idea I was always keeping for later – a street scene I'd spotted once in the blink of an eye one morning when I was up in London, but wanted to make so universal that the project just grew out of hand. In my mind it applies to any human relationship. Everything ends, one way or another. It could be day, it could be night, it could be any street in any city in the world. That's Everyman down the end of the road."

"And at the top, watching them go."

"Oh yes," Alexander picked up enthusiasm. "Sometimes the watcher and the walker are the same person. Often that street is the journey to let something go." He was silent for a moment, then said: "That's all life is, I suppose: an endless stream of things coming and going."

"And coming back," Felix stated.

Alexander smiled a knowing smile.

"Some of the best things come back. Sometimes though, the things that come back are the things you don't think you can handle, as if it's returned to test you. Sometimes those two things come back at once."

It remained silent for a moment. The wind from the open window blew a paper plate to the floor.

"Funny how a fresh pair of eyes can make you see your own work in a different light."

"Do you consider that legitimate?" Felix asked.

"I consider that the beauty of a painting – it can be anything to anyone. Come to think of it, that holds true for music, literature, dance, you name it. People will look at it through their own frame of reference. Of course they'll read something else into it than you will."

"But who then defines what the painting's about?"

"Well," said Alexander, "who's to say a painting can only convey one message? It's multi-faceted, it's always keeping

116

something concealed. The thing with art critics voicing their opinion is that it's precisely that, an *opinion*, based on their frame of reference."

"So it's a bit of a flexible truth?"

"I'd say so – within reason, of course. But if a person voices their honest thoughts on a piece, I can't possibly deny them their right to express that."

"What if someone says it's not art?" Felix asked.

"Then I inform them how mistaken they are about the very fundamentals of art and send them on their way."

"They must love that," Felix said.

"No, Felix," Alexander paused. "I speak from my own definition of art, which dictates that there's no viewer needed to confirm whether or not a painting, or a sculpture, whatever it is, is art. Art is art as soon as it's created. From its conception, there's only one thing it can be. It's in its DNA. A human will give birth to a new human being, an artist will give birth to art. It's so much about process that the thought you need others to decide for you whether or not it's art is ludicrous."

"But – then anyone can call anything art. Kick over a rubbish bin and call it art. Is it then, or is it not?"

"Of course it depends on the intent. If the person kicked it over to make a statement, say, in the middle of a pristine park to show...I don't know-" Alexander spread his arms, "that humans will destroy *anything* given enough time, then it's art."

Alexander moved over to his easel and held his hand up proudly.

"This is my latest piece," he said. In it, a couple sat in sunshine outside a café. Both faces were part-obscured. Those features that were visible were horribly transformed. In both their hands lay mobile phones, their gateway out of this world, their temporary pill of escapism before they had to engage with other humans again. "Human contact is dying," Alexander said, then moved back into the hall, where Felix saw more rows of canvases.

"Don't you sell any?" he asked.

"I do – these are mainly ones done for myself. For years after I left Vivienne, I felt a need to improve. It was a struggle to get back into painting after not doing much of it for years. It started with crippling self-doubt where I'd paint a picture and be so appalled at the result that I'd turn it to the wall and not paint again for weeks. Each brushstroke was a reminder of my insufficiency. Add to that the pressure that I now felt was on my painting after I'd burned all my other bridges and you get a pretty tough few years of my life. So I drank, hoping that would inspire me, loosen me up a little to create."

"And I'm guessing that worked wonders?" Felix asked.

"Course not. There's only so much that drink can do for you. What it gives with one hand in creativity and freedom, it snatches with the other in, well, general productivity."

Felix nodded.

"So for years I struggled to paint. Now, when I see the pieces I still have from that time, I don't hate them like I used to. Time has given me something of an objectivity towards them, a certain distance. They're now no longer time capsules of emotion. I can see them for their artistic merit."

"I did some writing yesterday," Felix said frankly, "and it felt just like that. I daren't even read it back. It seems to laugh in my face each time I do."

Alexander nodded. "Not uncommon, not uncommon at all. The trick is to break through that. I've broken through it in painting – I pay no heed to those thoughts. Ultimately, I'm painting for myself, not for anyone else."

"Until you are," Felix said.

"Well, yes. But that's a different kind of expression. Just remember – art is art from its conception. Anything you write as a direct consequence of life and thoughts is art, whether anyone else wants to read it or not. While beauty may be in the eye of the beholder, art is in the hand of the creator."

Felix found solace in Alexander's words. Though he may not have been a very good father, he was a seasoned artist, and that counted for more here.

"I'd be interested to read what you've written," Alexander continued.

Not just yet, Felix thought. It must've shown on his face, for Alexander said, "Not now, of course. Give it time. Give it confidence."

"Alright," Felix liked the prospect of having a guaranteed reader. It gave him something to write for and whether that was wrong or right, it motivated him.

"I always like reading a person's work. There's a side of the artist that comes through in writing more so than other art forms. If you read closely, you can see right into the artist's soul and get an understanding of the writer as a person."

Alexander seemed to remember something, got up and walked to the kitchen. Another overflowing ashtray stood amongst a forest of used mugs and reached for the bottle of rum. Cracking the neck, he pulled two mugs from the cupboard. So that's what all those mugs were from. They sat on Alexander's paint-spattered sofa, surveying the room, mugs in hand.

"You've produced a fair number," Felix said with a hint of admiration.

"This is all from the last two years. I sold much of what I had from before then to pay the bills. Some of them I put on the scrapheap. They weren't worth any better fate."

"What a waste," Felix found himself saying.

"Sometimes you have to make sacrifices. I was moving on, starting to experiment with a new style and the old stuff just didn't thrill me anymore. And when the art can't even excite the artist who made it, it's time for it to go. God knows where they are now."

"No," said Felix, "it's still a waste. You've thrown away the most legitimate record of process and of your progress that you'll ever have."

"Yes, but it just wasn't very good. I didn't want to look at it and it wasn't selling, so I had no choice. Sometimes you have to cut your losses."

Felix took a sip of rum, warm on his lips, throat and all the way down as it lined his stomach. He coughed briefly. Alexander reached into his pocket and pulled out a crumpled packet of cigarettes. He offered one to Felix, then held out the lighter. Felix inhaled and blew the smoke out into the room, where it hung briefly like a cloud.

"Do you see much of Roger?"

"A bit," said Alexander. "We used to meet now and then for a drink or three. Recently though all his time was taken up by a woman he met. She was good for him while it lasted. She pulled him up from the gutter he was in and fixed him up a bit."

"Oh?"

"Yeah," said Alexander. "He was in a bad way. He used to come out to the bar at 8pm, already completely plastered. Who he was drinking with I never found out. For weeks he walked the streets like a homeless man, sleeping rough on the odd night simply because he didn't care. It was a matter of inebriation rather than a lack of anywhere to go."

"Did you feel a certain responsibility?" Felix asked, "Seeing him in that state after being the one to convince him to come to Paris?"

"Is that what he said?" Alexander looked surprised. "I'm surprised he credits me with that much."

"So he said, 'back to the days of *Rogier et Alexandre*' was how he said you'd sold it to him."

"That's something I'd say," Alexander smirked.

"He wouldn't really tell me what that was all about," Felix said. "Something about dredging up old memories he said."

Alexander smiled. "There was a time when we were like brothers. We had such a strong connection and used to get through many a bottle of wine talking about everything from art to politics to society and our role in it. I don't think I've ever felt as powerfully creative as those days with Roger.

That freedom of thought, doing, *being*, not seen anywhere before or since, that rawness of life, that deep unexplainable confidence that what we were doing was right. The thought that there was not a single other thing we should be doing, but that, and there, and then. It was the most liberating time of my life." Alexander turned back to Felix with a start, as if remembering where he'd been going. "Anyway, on one of those days we started calling each other French names, and it sort of stuck."

"He mentioned you'd once been very close, but he didn't say much about it."

"Mmm, we really were. So of course I tried to help him up. I lent him money when I myself hardly had any. He slept on my sofa for weeks at a time. But whenever I took him out somewhere to get his mind off things, we'd end up drinking. I came to realise that all I was good for, was intoxicating myself and him, and that I couldn't really do anything more for him. At least his latest lady, Juliette I think her name was, gave him something to live for. Gave him the love he needed to pull himself out of his waking coma," he sighed, "but I guess eventually she'd had enough of trying to save a drowning soldier, and I heard from others that she gave him the boot recently, tired of swimming against the current. He's a great guy, but his knack for self-destruction exceeds even mine." Alexander looked around the room, at the ashtray and at his mug full of rum, and laughed. "Yes, that is indeed possible. Shouldn't laugh about it really, the deal I stumbled into with the devil. My long-term health for a sweet and consistent muse."

"Why do you do it to yourself then?"

"Don't try to tell me you don't drink too," retorted Alexander.

"Well, yes," Felix said, not sure whether to feel ashamed or proud.

"And do you create anything out of it?" Alexander prodded.

Broken hearts, a lot of the time, Felix thought, but instead just shook his head.

"I feel that as long as there's something creative coming out of it, it's not wasted self-destruction. Many of my canvases were painted under the influence of something."

"So it's not even really you painting it," Felix said.

"I disagree. It's almost more me than if I painted sober. It's almost as if I need the help getting it out, need something to distract me from the torture of getting the paintings finished."

"Which you find at the bottom of a bottle or at the burning tip of a cigarette." Felix concluded.

"Well, yes."

"It sounds like painting is a bit of a chore for you," Felix said.

"Hah, well that's one of life's great paradoxes," Alexander laughed. "'I don't always particularly like writing, but I always love having written.' That feeling of having created something in the real world that before only existed in my mind, the creation of something out of essentially nothing – a few inert tubes of paint and the hair of a dead animal."

"But after all this time, hasn't that won over the not

wanting to paint?" Felix asked.

"You'd have thought so. But I still have days, Felix, where I can't pick up my brush for fear of letting myself down, for fear of spoiling what's already there. I don't trust my own hand to create something my brain will be satisfied with. So I don't create at all, because what's not there can't be bad, right?"

"Right," said Felix.

"Wrong," said Alexander. "What's not there, is emptiness, untouched, unspoken. And that's worse than something you paint but are unhappy with. The onus is always on creation, because not creating leaves you feeling so helpless and miserable. The only thing, in my mind, worse than painting badly, is not painting at all. That's when I'll really be pulled down – not after a day of frustrated paint-mixing and daubing. At least then I'll have produced."

"But, why this..." Felix searched for the right word, "compulsion, to create? Sometimes the best things in life come to nothing. Why try to force the issue?"

"Because that way, I have made something that may induce a feeling in another, somehow. I have expressed myself. I may therefore be understood, now and many years into the future. If I hold my tongue with no words spoken and not a single brushstroke on the canvas, I am dumb – a mute behind closed gates. It's a language, definitely."

"You speak it well," Felix offered.

"Well, each day brings a different perceived level of artistic proficiency. I've met plenty of Parisians who aren't confident enough to speak English for fear of making mistakes. That's how I sometimes feel with art." He exhaled exaggeratedly, as if recognising he'd gone on too long. The light was fading outside, and the sky had turned a dirty blue, flecked by the clouds.

"You remember Sylvene?" Alexander asked.

How could he not?

"Her band is playing at a jazz bar in town later tonight. Beautiful voice. You fancy going?"

"Sure."

"Great," Alexander said. "We can get some food on the way."

Girls' laughter from the street below broke the silence of the room.

"Let's go," said Alexander.

*

The food he spoke of was from a small hole in the wall with steaming dishes standing around on hot plates. This vendor too, Alexander knew. They found a bench and sat eating off their knees. Felix felt a sense of pride in being so far outside his mother's usual world of sit-down meals and knife-and-fork diplomacy.

When they'd finished, they dropped the tubs into a bin and walked in the direction of the jazz bar. The band was tuning up when they arrived. Of Sylvene there was no sign yet.

"She'll swan in as the gig is due to start and wonder what everyone was fretting about," Alexander said. Sonny Rollins played on speakers older than Felix was and a solitary disco lamp blinked at the wall behind the performers. It was a bit of a sad place, Felix thought, but beers were cheap and Alexander had promised crowds. Sylvene rocked up as expected, five minutes before the band was going to start, then took an age to join them. There was no stage to speak of, just a space on the floor for a drumkit and precious little else, with the other musicians crammed into the corner. You had to walk so close past them to go to the toilet that you could feel the wind from the saxophone and almost touch the double-bassist. Sylvene considered herself above a soundcheck, as she made her way slowly over to the podium, stopping to kiss and chat to nigh on every person in the room. Alexander was not left out. She spoke animatedly, bringing life to the dreary bar. She kissed Alexander on both cheeks, then approached Felix.

"Everysing ok?" she asked. Felix found her accent intriguing.

"Yes thanks," he said, while leaning in for a two-cheek peck. He smelt spirits on her, spirits and scent. She moved away and rolled up her coat, once bright-red but aged by years of abuse, into a ball and tossed it into the corner where it lay like a beacon on the floor. She then walked over to the band. Used to her diva's entrance, they paid her minimal notice before the saxophonist piped up a melancholy stream of notes and filled the small bar with sadness. As the double bassist and drummer joined in, Sylvene signalled to them, then disappeared off to the bar. The drummer rolled his eyes but kept playing, drawing out the instrumental for several minutes while Sylvene took her time, getting a drink the barman wouldn't let her pay for. Ambling back from the bar during the sax solo, she stood in front of the old full-metal mic, cradling it in her hand. Felix finished his beer and went to the bar for two more. A beer in a brown bottle high up on a shelf caught his eye and he pointed to them, signalling two. The barman took two Westmalle Dubbel out of a fridge and opened them, their caps coming free with a satisfying fizz. Felix put the two squat goblets down on the table in front of Alexander, who looked pleasantly surprised. He returned to the bar for the bottles and to pay.

At that point Sylvene started singing. Her voice fitted along with the jazz like a fifth instrument. It filled the gaps between the piano's fragile notes, rose above the medley of double-bass and saxophone and played beautiful love games with the drummer's syncopation. Her voice dancing along the bars brought colour to this bar, painting over all the cracks and signs of age, for once making it young again. It probably had the same effect on some of the older folk in the bar, rolling back the years in wave after wave of nostalgia. Oh, to be in a jazz bar in Paris, Felix thought, suddenly immensely happy. He sat down again on the barstool, never taking his eyes off Sylvene. She seemed to inhabit a world of her own, carried on the shoulders of the musicians like royalty, waving at her adulators. As her show continued, Felix was lifted higher again, a combination of alcohol and total immersion in the sound, to places far away from where he sat. He stood on a railway platform, a train to some far-off city ahead of him, high iron arches towering overhead. He felt the surge of freedom of being, the liberty of movement and existence anywhere in the world. His eyes and mind were open as he watched Sylvene round off her slice of vocal magic and heard himself applauding. Sylvene smiled sweetly from the stage, dropping a little curtsy. She looked and sounded like a diva, somehow out of place in this dive, an angel come down from heaven to shed light on a dreary scene before she'd be off to work her magic someplace else.

The piece came to an end. Applause from the crowd came in spatters. The saxophonist came forward and introduced the band. The next piece they would play, he announced, was called *La Ritournelle*. Sylvene took a seat at the bar and sipped at her wine. The drummer, double bassist and piano started off on a beat that was reminiscent of a playground game of hopscotch. The mood grew lighter and lighter, a real springtime chanson, while Felix walked springtime streets in his mind, with nowhere to be and no time to be there. He sauntered over pavements, down the middle of suburban roads which saw no cars, past gardens bursting into bloom.

Spring air, spring in the step, he thought to himself, the words pressing at his mind to be written down and committed to history immediately, but he wasn't ready to come down yet, too absorbed in the music to be snapped out of it. He felt a cool breeze on his face, cooling and cleansing as when he'd stood by Senna's open window. It carried the scent of life restarting after a harsh winter, bedroom windows open for the first time in months and the world opening up again for business.

Sylvene moved back towards the musicians and stood

swaying, eyes closed, by the mic stand. She was not necessarily the most attractive of girls, her dark hair hanging loose around her shoulders and her appearance bordering on scruffy, save for a flash of red lipstick. It belied her diva's behaviour. She kept her eyes closed, but started singing of a romance, a romance that could only take place in summer, of tumbling in high grass, consumed by each others' love and needing nothing else but that. The guitarist joined the party, fast, high-pitched notes flooding from the belly of his guitar, then died down again, leaving the piano, double bass and drums to carry the tune downwards into a slow death in winter. As the music dropped from the air, Felix looked around in disbelief that all this had happened in this very bar, the epitome of brow-broken backstreet bars. Applause came again in showers of drizzle. Maybe this crowd of regulars was spoilt, having heard this a hundred times before, and more. Felix didn't think this could ever get old, eternal youth through music. Maybe that was what kept bringing people back.

Throughout the next four songs, Sylvene grew in brilliance, until it was almost as if an aura hung around her. She'd ascended from a plain girl to a vocal goddess, and now Felix couldn't shake that image. He hadn't spoken a word to Alexander since the music had started, hadn't even looked round at him. Now he did, he found him hunched over a notebook with a pencil in his hand, the lines on the page depicting the lamp hanging over the musicians, a conical object which caught the light and shot it up itself like a golden path. Felix hadn't even noticed the lamp, so absorbed had he been by what was going on underneath it. Alexander had captured not only the shining path to perfection with only two colours, but also caught the grain of the brushed aluminium, even bending it around a small dent on the left-hand side. It was astonishing how accurate Alexander's drawing was. What was more, it gave the lamp a personality and a back-story, all through debris left behind on a page. It was so atmospheric that it told the story of how the lamp had got dented, how long it had hung there and all the creation and destruction it had watched over. Alexander had given it a personality. Felix leaned over and tapped the table by Alexander's book. At first Alexander didn't look up, absorbed in getting the slope of the light just right, but after a few more strokes he put the pencil in his mouth and looked up.

The saxophonist announced the next song as *"Pieces"*. Sylvene started almost immediately over what Felix would more readily classify as funk, a swinging, downbeat tune that matched Sylvene's words of heartbreak and alcohol that Felix immediately related to Alexander's telling of Roger's story. The song built in intensity as Sylvene wailed her song of pain into the microphone, rising higher and higher to the crescendo as the sax blew chunks of hurt into the air and the drummer drummed himself into a melancholy-fuelled madness, the sound filling the bar and likely spilling out, leaving not a person in this city untouched, a wall of sound crashing down in a rain of bricks and perfectly-timed cacophony: *"Picking pieces,"* she soared into the night air, crying out to the stars for the unfairness of it all, for the romance slowly burning away in a balance of love and utter destruction.

"Picking pieces off the ground," she concluded, bringing an end to the crescendo and coming back to Earth where she shrank back into the body that stood at the microphone. The musicians brought the piece to an end. Felix blinked in disbelief at the journey it had taken him on. He'd completely forgotten Alexander again, so it came as a surprise when Alexander tapped him on his bare arm with his pencil. Catching sight of the drawing on Alexander's page, by now finished, dated and signed, Felix remembered what he'd meant to say, but his mind didn't want to let go of the waking dreams he'd had along the bars and over the notes of the past half-hour.

"That was —" he broke off, looking for the right word.

"I know," said Alexander, "some of the best I've heard here. And I've been coming a long time."

"I was far away," Felix found himself repeating the line from when they'd been by the Seine.

"That's immersion for you." Alexander replied with a knowing smile, then turned his page over to a blank one.

"That lamp is amazing," Felix said.

"It's alright. I made a few mistakes," Alexander said. Felix hadn't noticed a damn thing wrong with it, and said so. Alexander just smiled.

"Do you have a pen on you?" Felix asked.

Alexander reached into his pocket and pulled one out. "Hope it still works," he said.

He smiled as Felix pulled out his notebook, still in pristine condition, pages not yet thickened by thoughts.

Spring in the air, spring in the step, Felix wrote, then pondered and wrote below it: *Spring in the air and step. Spring, heavy on the air, light on the step. On the step of spring in the air. Spring upon us, light in the step*, refining his words with every iteration. None yet seemed quite right. He put the book aside, folding it closed over the pen, and turned to his nearly untouched beer. It tasted exactly how the colour brown would, dark and hoppy, rich, chocolatey, muddy but not unpleasant. Struck again, he started writing, his experiences of long-distance travel through music now translated to words – each art form really was its own language, and as you were born with a mothertongue, so too perhaps are people born with a mother-art. Or some weren't born with any at all, Felix realised. Starved of art and appreciation for creativity all their lives, without even realising it, busying themselves on other fronts, seeking beauty elsewhere and in doing so, freeing themselves from the shackles of art he had discovered through his own writings and Alexander's insight into the world of art, freeing them from artistic insecurity, self-doubt, hate for that very thing that they are. It would be a pleasant life, Felix thought, but a shallow one. It took him a moment to realise that was the life he'd been living up to that point and the admission came so suddenly he had no chance to reject it. He felt a warm expansion of ego as he thought of his growth, and a starry-eyed anticipation as to what was still to come. By the time he put his pen down, three sides of paper had been filled with truth – absolute truth he knew, for he had felt it and expressed it. Was this then art, in Alexander's sense of the word? Purest art as expressed direct from the soul to the paper, almost bypassing the muscular system but for enslaving it to write, to get those words down on paper in the order they needed to be put in. He took another sip from his beer. Alexander coughed, renewing Felix's awareness of the bar they sat in, poky without the music now the musicians had gone on break.

Over the course of the next three hours, the music continued to bring meaning to the otherwise drab bar. As the fresh beers came cold out of the tap and disappeared into thirsty jazzfolk, the crowd growing every time Felix looked up from his book, so too did the outside world start to matter less and less – the here and now faded to become purely conversation and mad jazz. There was no outside, there were no jobs, daily life was all a dream. High up on his barstool, the music acted as a vehicle for Felix's thoughts, drawing them out and turning them over in its enlightened, nimble hands. People came and went outside of Felix's span of consciousness. He sat, reading back what he'd written, until a hand came and gestured to put the book aside.

"Don't read it back," Felix realised the hand was Alexander's as was the voice accompanying it. "You'll only beat yourself up. Read it in the morning."

Would any of it even make sense in the morning?

The musicians had finished their final set now, and were packing up and milling around the emptying bar. Sylvene came over, and Felix gushed praise at her and the performance she'd just turned in. She soaked it up, basking in it almost more than being on stage.

Felix and Alexander left the bar soon after. Far off, echoes of a clock striking two reached them on the breeze. It had clearly rained while they were inside, and after weeks of dry, the rain pulled a dusty smell out of the roads. From down the street crept more music, more minimal this time. It grew louder until the pair reached a bus stop, where two people sat, the man on accordion, the woman with a violin. Like a nimble gymnast, the violin danced the melody, leaving the accordion in charge of the rhythm of the piece. They found a bench on the square nearby and sat watching, like a cooling-down exercise after heavy exertion. Wet cobblestones reflected the light coming out of *Au Clarion des Chasseurs*, where three couples still sat drinking under terrace heaters. Just around the corner, refusing to pay outrageous prices for a glass of wine at the café, four young men perched on a stranger's steps, passing a bottle around and revelling in the music. Each time a piece of music came to an end, applause rose from this casual audience. The violinist curtseyed.

It seemed to Felix that along one of the main arteries of Parisian tourism, they'd chanced upon a pocket of 1950's life, as if stepping into an old painting. A stroller came by, a woman. She sat down next to the musicians and piped up at times, telling ditties of a life through song. After the one song, she shook hands with the musicians and headed off into the night. Spontaneous, absurd and free.

As Felix left, Alexander suggested they do something tomorrow.

"I'll call you, no idea what time I'll be up."

"Sure. Goodnight."

"Night!"

He was awoken by the phone ringing in his room. 8:13 blinked at him from the alarm clock. He picked up the phone and grunted. The voice on the other side was prim and polished. The hotel reception.

"Would you like to stay another night, sir?"

Felix was annoyed. He'd been booking and paying for his stay one night at a time since a few days into his trip. Why would it be different now?

"Yes," replied Felix, "I'll come down."

Now he was awake, he might as well get it over with, then go back to sleep. His head throbbed. Pulling on a pair of jeans and a t-shirt, with a cap to hide his messy locks, he proceeded downstairs with his wallet in his right hand, the bannister in his left for support. The receptionist was serving another lady, pointing out something or other on a map, so Felix took a seat in one of the leather armchairs in the lobby. It was a white marble affair – or some faux marble, judging by the price of the room – the look of an owner who wanted an upscale hotel but didn't want to spend the money getting it. The receptionist finished with the lady and she swung the door to the street open, issuing a friendly "*Merci!*" at the receptionist who smiled and bowed his head. Felix approached the desk.

"Another night, sir?"

"Mmm." Felix muttered.

"How would you like to pay?"

Felix held up his card. In his foggy state he'd pulled out his driving licence, but the man knew what he meant. He typed in the price as Felix dug for his debit card. "49.00" flashed up on the screen. Felix inserted his card and entered his pin. It beeped back at him, long and angry. "Payment not accepted" it read. The receptionist read the puzzled look on Felix's face and suggested he try again. When the message showed up the second time, the receptionist read out the receipt to Felix. "Insufficient balance". Felix's heart sank. This whole trip he'd not thought of money at all, safe in the knowledge he had more than enough to last through his time. But hotel nights and evenings of drinking had taken their toll on his bank account. He was thrown, for a minute completely unsure as to what to do. Could he get more? Only through Vivienne, and she wouldn't be keen. Slowly, he came to realise this as a sign, an indication that it was time to be heading off.

"Okay," he said resignedly. "I'll leave today."

Check-out was at 11am, so Felix stripped off and went back to bed again. He tossed and turned and couldn't get comfortable, dilemma tearing at his mind between heart and wallet. How he'd love to stay, explore more of this city with Alexander, see Senna again. But he knew he couldn't. He resigned himself to the fact he couldn't sleep, to the fact he was leaving, and made for the shower.

After he'd packed, he called Alexander.

"I have to leave," he said, heavy-heartedly.

"I can lend you money," Alexander said after Felix had

recounted the story.

Felix battled again in his mind.

"No, thanks. It's time I left."

"Let's get a coffee before you go."

"Let me book my bus and see what time I've got."

"Let me know," Alexander said.

Felix took the metro to *Gare de l'Est* and queued up at the ticket office. Had he known Paris? he wondered to himself. To an extent. He'd met Parisians and strayed off the tired tourist track. He'd seen the Eiffel Tower, from a distance. He'd jilted the Mona Lisa.

The next bus was pulling out at quarter past midday and Felix reckoned it safest to get a seat on it. The fare took a fair chunk of his remaining money. He dialled Alexander.

"My bus leaves in an hour and a half."

"Where are you now?" Alexander asked.

"*Gare de l'Est.*"

"By the time I got there, you'd almost have left. Well Felix, then it's farewell. Thanks for coming to visit." Alexander sounded choked. "Thanks for persisting and overcoming my wall of shame. I hope our paths cross again soon. You have become a man, my son."

It was strange to hear Alexander call him that – even to hear Alexander's voice like that. Felix wasn't the only one moved by the journey.

Felix sat down on a metal rail, back to the pillar holding up the roof of the station. He pulled out a book and reveled in the sun's rays, content to pass the time reading. He'd not properly read for over a week, consumed by other sides of artistic life and engaged with the city. Now he could take a step back and let it all sink in, his eyes reading the flowing prose but his thoughts in a million places, running through where he'd been this week, feeling the notebook in his coat pocket as tangible proof of his growth and the prospect of returning to the city again soon. He'd hardly thought of Vivienne since his revelation in the Louvre – thought of her world and all she symbolised, yes, but never directly of her. What a week, a week he could not even imagine a week ago. It just went to show, in hindsight the future was impossible to predict. He checked his watch. His bus left in half an hour. He got up, grabbed his bag and went to see where it left from. Finding the platform, but finding it languishing in the shade, he went back outside to where he had been sitting. As he went to sit down, he spotted a mop of brown hair coming down the street. Alexander? Felix was hit with a wave of pleasant surprise to see him again, to know he'd gone out of his way to get here. The two acknowledged each other at a distance, and Felix got up and embraced Alexander.

"I couldn't not see you again," Alexander said. "Thanks for making the trip, it means so much to me. I'm glad we could patch a few things up."

"It's been good," Felix agreed. Then eventually added: "I've seen your side."

"Look, Felix, it's not about *my* side. It's about a decision I took to put myself first and pursue an art form I just can't do without. And you want to know something?"

Felix remained quiet in anticipation.

"I still miss your mother so much."

Felix was only moderately surprised by this.

"But I know there's not a bone in her body left untouched by what I did that would allow her to take me back. In the long run, it wouldn't do me any good anyway. It didn't last time." Alexander shook his head. It seemed to Felix that he'd made peace with it, that his trip and his bringing it back into Alexander's consciousness had rounded off a long-standing feud in his mind, closed off that book.

"Well – I admire it." Felix said.

"And I admire you," Alexander said, reaching into his coat pocket to bring out something oblong and wrapped. "I got this for you."

As Felix unwrapped it, bright paper made way for hard leather, and when he opened the case, inside nestled a dark red pen, its metal features glinting in the sun. Felix drew breath.

"To my son, the writer." Alexander said.

Felix was struck dumb by the gesture. He put his free arm around Alexander, pulling him in close.

"Thank you," he said.

"Now go out and make something of it," Alexander said.

"I don't have a choice," Felix blinked back tears.

"No," agreed Alexander. "True artists never do."

Felix checked his watch. Five minutes to departure. The pair got up and hugged again, standing against the sun, flanked as silhouettes beside the station and tall buildings.

"Take care son," Alexander said.

"I will," Felix said, "I will, Dad."

Alexander turned away so Felix couldn't see the tears on his cheeks. He walked straight out of the station and straight to the metro.

Felix found his bus and boarded it. He sat down, still baffled by the week just gone. As the bus pulled out of the station, he started writing.

> *as blue sky morning greets the wrong end of night*
> *waves of a smile crease tear-streaked cheeks*
> *roll and lap the bank, crash and pull back*
> *like hesitation rising from crumpled sheets*
> *all we are is fresh air and empty streets.*